Gathering of Pearls

Gathering of Pearls

Written by
Sook Nyul Choi

Houghton Mifflin Company
Boston

Text copyright © 1994 by Sook Nyul Choi

www.houghtonmifflinbooks.com

Gathering of pearls / by Sook Nyul Choi.
p.   cm.
Summary: Sookan struggles to balance her new life as a college fresh-
man in the United States with expectations from her family at home
in Korea.
HC ISBN: 0-395-67437-9   PB ISBN: 0-618-80918-X
[1. Universities and collges—Fiction. 2. Koreans—United States—
Fiction.]
I. Title.
PZ7.C44626Gat 1994   94-10868
[Fic]—dc20   CIP   AC

HC ISBN-13: 978-0-395-67437-6
PA ISBN-13: 978-0-618-80918-9

Printed in the United States of America
BP 10 9 8 7 6 5 4 3 2 1

To Audrey, writer and voyager

By the Author

Novels
Year of Impossible Goodbyes
Echoes of the White Giraffe
Gathering of Pearls

Picture Books
Halmoni and the Picnic

Acknowledgments

My thanks to Kathy for her support and input in every step of the manuscript's evolution, and to John for his enthusiasm and interest. Many thanks to Audrey for her loving encouragement and critiques. And, as always, my sincere thanks to Lauri for her guidance and continued support of my work.

Sook Nyul Choi
Cambridge, 1994

Gathering of Pearls

Chapter One

September 1954

Would I ever get out of the belly of this giant metal bird? It had been a long flight across the Pacific, and we had already made stopovers in Anchorage and Seattle. It had been twenty-eight hours since I left Seoul, and the flight still seemed endless. My legs ached from sitting so long, and my head throbbed. Everyone around me had fallen asleep, but my mind kept racing.

I had been so determined to leave Korea and study in America, but now that I was on the plane, I felt nervous. I remembered how I had pestered our priest, Father Lee, to help me. He had finally gone to the bishop to talk about me, and the bishop had put Father Lee in touch with a nun he knew at Finch College, an all-girls Catholic college in New York. How excited I had been when I heard back from the college that I had been granted a scholarship. But my mother, Father Lee, and my four brothers thought I was too young to go so far away.

Now, suddenly, I worried that maybe they were right. I knew no one in America, and my command of English was poor. Would I understand people there, and would they be able to understand me? How would I keep up with all the American students at college? Would they like me? Would I like them?

Finally, the pilot announced that we were about to land at Idlewild Airport in New York. As I watched everyone begin moving about, collecting their things, I was seized with a strange blend of anxiety and excitement. This was it. I was finally in America with my new life ahead of me. Half dazed from the sleepless night, I made my way through immigration and customs, following the bustling crowds.

Everything around me seemed larger than life. The terminal was huge, and all the people were so big and tall. I looked around and saw no one who looked nineteen years old, as I was. For a minute, I wished I belonged to one of the older travelers in front of me. But I just kept on walking, propelled by the sea of people. The burly men ahead of me were speaking loudly in English, and I strained to see if I could understand what they were saying. They bantered back and forth, sometimes bursting out laughing and slapping each other on the back. I understood a few words here and there, but they spoke too quickly for me to comprehend what they were talking about. I wondered how I would ever manage to get through college.

As I walked through the swinging doors, I saw a crowd eagerly awaiting the arrival of our flight. People began waving and shouting, then rushing toward each other with kisses and open arms. How wonderfully warm these people were. I had never seen anyone embrace and kiss in public like this. In Korea, we bowed deeply to greet each other. I wondered if the students meeting me would hug me. Would I know the right way to hug them back?

Clutching my black patent leather purse and my little suitcase, I anxiously looked right and left for a group of college students waving red hearts. Two days before I left Seoul, I had received a letter from the dean of students saying that a couple of my classmates would meet me at the airport. They would be waving large, red felt hearts; it was a long-standing tradition of the college to greet new students this way. I had been envisioning this moment ever since I read the letter. I imagined a band of pretty girls, all waving hearts, rushing toward me as I stepped off the plane. But as I stopped to look around, I saw no red hearts and no girls my age.

I searched the crowd anxiously, trying to smile and hide my mounting fears. I did not even have directions to the college. All I had was the address and phone number. The crowd was dwindling, and I stared at the glass doors, hoping to see someone rushing in to find me. I tried to comfort myself, thinking perhaps they were just late. But the area was almost empty now. I felt so alone in the huge airport. I would just wait, I decided.

I straightened my gray wool dress that Mother had designed and made for me. It was a simple but fashionable dress with three small bows down the front which hid the buttons. Mother had a good sense of style and sewed very well. "When your American friends first see you, I want them to know that you have simple, yet good taste — with a touch of flair," Mother had said with quiet satisfaction as she sewed on the last bow. "A black patent leather purse and matching pumps, and you will look just fine." The memory of Mother's soothing voice rang in my ears. I was glad she was not here to see me standing all alone in this big, empty airport, feeling scared and unwanted.

After waiting almost an hour and a half, I just could not wait any longer. I got up and headed for the public phone booth. Jaechun, my second oldest brother, had given me some American coins that he had saved. I carefully read all the instructions on the pay phone, inserted a few coins, and embarked on my first telephone conversation in English.

"Hello, this is Sookan Bak. I come from Seoul, Korea," I said slowly, with my voice trembling. "Sister Casey, the freshman dean, is there, please?"

"Oh, dear, a lost freshman!" answered a welcoming voice. "You are mighty late! No one is around right now. They are all in the assembly hall for the final orientation session. Just a minute, please. Let me see if I can reach Sister Casey."

As I waited, a recording came on, telling me to insert more change. I frantically dug through my purse and added the last of the coins Jaechun had given me, praying I would not have to wait much longer for Sister Casey.

4

"Hello. Yes, Sister Casey says it is best if you come straight over as you are already so late. She will meet you in front of the administration building. It's called 'The Castle.' "

"I am at Idlewild Airport. Can you please tell me how I can go to Finch College? Can you please tell me slowly?" I asked.

Struggling to understand, I wrote down everything she said. Outside the terminal, I found the big bus to Grand Central Station, just as it was about to drive away. I waved wildly, got on the bus, and settled in for the ride. We sped by rows and rows of New York City skyscrapers, but I felt too overwhelmed to appreciate anything so new and different.

At Grand Central Station, throngs of people rushed to and fro with determination. I stood in the middle of the crowds and stared at the long row of ticket counters, trying to decipher the many signs. I finally found the right ticket booth and, after waiting in a long line, bought my ticket and boarded the train to White Plains.

Contrary to what the college operator had said, this was quite a long trip, and I was terribly afraid of getting lost. But I got off at White Plains Station, as I had been instructed, and got into a taxi. My head throbbed. My life in this new country was not starting out as I had expected. Would everything be such a struggle for me here? I sat on the edge of my seat, clutching the sheet of paper on which I had written the directions. I watched the meter click as we sped down the maze of unfamiliar roads, and I softly asked how much farther we had to go. The driver smiled kindly and told me to sit back and relax.

We finally turned onto a smaller road that headed up a lush, green hill. At the top, there was a large, gray stone structure with four turrets, just like the pictures in the book of *King Arthur's Tales* that I had read. *No wonder they call the administration building The Castle,* I thought to myself as I let out a huge sigh of relief.

As the taxi pulled to a stop, a tall nun approached. I quickly stepped out of the taxi, and before I had a chance to bow, she opened her arms and hugged me tightly. Her arms locked around my trembling body and her voice rang. "Sookan, hello. I am Sister Casey, your class dean and theology professor. My heavens! All alone, all the way from Korea! I am terribly sorry there was a mix-up about your arrival date."

Her long black veil fell around my shoulders, encasing me in a soothing darkness. There was an odd smell about her, a mingling of antiseptic and sweat, which I somehow found comforting. When she released me from her tight embrace, I stood awkwardly before her, staring down at my purse. It was strangely disconcerting for me not to be bowing. I wondered how I was supposed to show my respect for her.

She bent down to look into my eyes and said with a concerned smile, "Well, I'm sorry you missed orientation week, but I'm glad you're here safe and sound. It'll be all right. We'll get you settled in." I could almost hear her thinking, *The one who needs orientation week the most, and here she is, the last one to arrive.*

With a helpless smile, I apologized and explained that my visa had come late. She cheerfully told me not to worry, and asked me if I wanted to rest. Formulating my response in my head, careful to put the words in the right order, I slowly answered that I wasn't tired, and that I wanted to meet my classmates. She seemed concerned, but said with a smile, "Well, in that case, how about changing into your native costume and we can surprise everyone at the assembly hall."

I wished I could refuse. I preferred to meet everyone in my Western clothes. I didn't want to attract so much attention to myself. But instead I heard myself meekly responding, "Yes, Sister Casey." I couldn't say no to an elder's request.

She escorted me to a small empty room in The Castle and said, "When you are ready, come down the hall to my office and we will go over to the assembly hall together. You may leave all your belongings in there for now. Hurry, so you can catch Sister Reed's speech."

In the cold room, I opened my suitcase and pulled out a pale blue silk *hanbok*. The crisp dress that Mother had packed so carefully was now all wrinkled from the long journey in my tiny suitcase. Mother would be upset if she knew I was showing up at the assembly hall wearing a wrinkled *hanbok*. I sighed, but got myself ready in a hurry.

"Oh, you look absolutely enchanting!" Sister Casey

said when she saw me standing in front of her office. "It will be such a treat for everyone. And it must make you feel at home to be in your native dress."

I just smiled as I gathered part of the skirt, the *chima*, in my hands and took careful steps down the stairs. I did not feel comfortable; I felt awkward and self-conscious. I already looked so different from everyone with my black hair and yellow skin that I didn't want to make myself stand out even more. I would have liked to slip in quietly at the back of the assembly hall and have a chance to observe unnoticed. But when I entered the packed room, all heads turned. My face burned with embarrassment. I didn't know what to do, and instinctively just bowed. I felt like a rare bird on display, and at that moment, I wished I had a pair of invisible wings that would carry me far, far away.

A girl's voice rang out, lifting the heavy air around me. "Oh, Sister Casey, Sookan is my roommate. I've been waiting for her. Sookan, sit next to me. I'm so glad you're finally here!" The tall, blond freshman with the blue eyes and winning smile beckoned. Relieved, I quickly rushed over and took the seat next to her. "Hi, my name is Ellen — Ellen Lloyd," she whispered. "You're so beautiful!"

"How did you know my name?" I asked.

"I saw your picture in the freshman file that Sister Casey has in her office," she said.

I was grateful to Ellen and I admired her outgoing

nature. I sat back in my chair and began listening to Sister Reed.

"Sunday through Thursday, you must all be in your rooms by ten o'clock, and lights must be out by the ten-fifteen bell. Weekend curfew is eleven P.M. and is strictly enforced. It is important that you abide by the dorm rules; anyone who violates these rules will receive the appropriate number of demerits. Ten demerits, and you will not be allowed off campus the following weekend. Now, with regard to male visitors: men are only to be received in the sitting room on the first floor of each dormitory. Under no circumstances are they allowed upstairs. Male visitors must be off campus by nine-thirty P.M. on weekdays, and by eleven o'clock on weekends."

As the speech continued, Ellen whispered to me, "I hear Sister Reed has bright red hair. See how red her eyebrows are? They say she was a cheerleader in high school, and that all the boys chased her. Can you imagine!" Her expression was animated and cheerful. "Here, everyone is afraid of her. She is the vice president of the college, and is very strict. She teaches a course on marriage to the seniors, and they say she's tough. But they also say that if she decides she likes you, there's nothing she won't do for you."

With renewed respect, I listened to Sister Reed. I couldn't keep my eyes off her red eyebrows and her green eyes that sparkled like emeralds.

Later that evening, when we were alone in our room,

Ellen watched me rush into the bathroom to change into a Western skirt and blouse. "Oh no, now you look just like everyone else here," she said. "I wanted you to stay in your Korean outfit longer. You looked so pretty and special."

I wanted to tell her how ill at ease I felt in that long, foreign outfit. I wished I could explain to her that I didn't want to be special just because I looked different. I longed to blend in so that I could learn to be part of the new world around me. But as I silently tried to formulate these thoughts into coherent English sentences, I saw Ellen staring at me and knew I had to respond.

"Thank you for liking my dress," I simply blurted out. "It is called a *hanbok*. But I am more comfortable in these." I pointed to my simple skirt and blouse. It was just too hard to express myself in English. English grammar was almost the complete opposite of the Korean. I wondered how long it would be before I could voice my thoughts and feelings accurately and freely. It was so frustrating to speak using such simple words. I probably sounded like a baby, and I worried that Ellen and the others would think me slow and stupid. I blushed and pretended to be absorbed in unpacking.

Ellen watched me in silence for a while and then began to help. Methodically, she hung and folded my things. As we worked, she asked me many simple questions, such as my birthday, my age, what the weather is like in Korea, and what type of food we eat there. She seemed to understand everything I said, and she smiled so warmly at me that I began to relax about making grammatical mistakes, and just talked and talked.

She unwrapped the picture frame with the photo of my family, and placed it on my dresser. "Where is your father?" she asked, after I had pointed out my mother, my older sister, and my four brothers.

"He died during the Korean War," I said rather uncomfortably.

"Oh, Sookan, I'm sorry," Ellen said. "Where did you take this picture? Is that Seoul? It looks so serene there."

"That was at the convent. We all went to see my sister there that day."

"You look awfully serious in this picture, Sookan," Ellen observed as she examined the photo.

"I had been talking to my sister. She told me she did not want me to come to America. She said I was too young to come by myself. She had plans for me in Korea," I murmured, remembering the lecture I had received that day. Not wanting to think about this anymore, I glanced over at the picture on Ellen's bureau, which was right next to mine. I had been wondering about the boy in that picture.

Ellen immediately reached for it to show me. "This is Kyle, my boyfriend. I met him a year ago, through my cousin, and we took this picture last spring when I was visiting him at Princeton. I can't wait till we're married. I already know that I want us to live in a yellow house with green shutters. And I want us to have four children, two boys and two girls."

I was at once stunned and impressed by all her plans. I had never heard anyone speak this way about marriage. In Korea, girls don't talk about such things. There, marriage is an event that is left to the elders to arrange and decide upon.

The bell rang loudly as a cue for us to turn the light out. The bustling dorm suddenly fell quiet and dark. As we lay in our beds, Ellen told me more about Kyle. He was a junior at Princeton majoring in economics, and an only child like herself. Her voice faded into the distance as I drifted off to sleep after my long journey.

Chapter Two

The next day, at Ellen's urging, the two of us took the college bus to downtown White Plains. Ellen wanted us to buy matching curtains, bedspreads, and accessories for our room, so we headed straight for the "home accessories department" at Bonwit Teller's. Ellen immediately pointed to a set of bright pink curtains trimmed with lace, and to their matching accessories. "Don't you like this one?"

"Yes, I don't like it," I replied, noticing the high price tag. What little pocket money I had brought from home would be almost gone if I bought this. I had already spent a lot on transportation yesterday, and I still needed to buy books for class. It had been hard for Mother to save the small sum she had given me when I left. My airplane ticket and the clothes and other things Mother had bought for me had cost a great deal. I think Mother borrowed money from our relatives to pay for these things, and I knew she and my brothers would not be able to send me any more money from home. As a scholarship student, the college covered my tuition, and room and board. In return, however, I was to work fifteen hours a week in the college dining hall as scholarship work, and was required to earn good grades in all my courses and to meet the social, moral, and religious standards of the school. I would have to figure out some way to earn pocket money on the side.

"Sookan, what do you mean?" Ellen asked, looking very puzzled. " 'Yes, you like it' or 'no, you don't like it.' Which is it?"

"I mean I do *not* like it," I said, sorry to be disagreeable. I felt embarrassed, and worried that I had hurt her feelings. I wondered why Ellen had asked me what I meant. Then, as she busily searched for another pattern, I realized that I had made a mistake when answering her. I was still thinking in Korean. No wonder she was confused!

I smiled at my own mistake and said, "Ellen, I am sorry that my answer was confusing to you. I am trying to speak in English, but my thoughts are still in Korean. In Korean, the proper way to answer your question is to say 'Yes, you are right that I do not like it.' It is confusing for me to keep all the English grammar rules straight. I am sorry I did not like your choice."

"Oh, don't worry. If you don't like it, just say no, no matter how the question is asked. English is simple!"

But it was not simple. Everything seemed so different here — not only the language, but the way of thinking, too.

"Come on," Ellen said, "I'm sure we can find something we both like." I felt like giving her a hug. Instead, I busied myself looking at various curtains and desk sets. Ellen seemed to like bright colors, so I suggested a print that had a bright floral pattern against a beige background. Ellen was pleased, and we picked out everything to match, even the wastebasket. Color coordination seemed a serious matter to Ellen. Her outfits matched right down to her nail polish and earrings. I wondered what Ellen must think of me, in my simple gray skirt, white blouse, and functional loafers.

I was eager to return to school to look at the course catalog, but Ellen insisted that we stop for sodas. As we sat drinking our ginger ales, other college students that Ellen knew came in, and she introduced me to all of them. They were upperclassmen that Ellen had met during orientation week. They had come up to school early to help the incoming freshmen. Ellen showed them all the things we had bought, and they congratulated us on our wonderful choices. How comfortable they all were talking to each other. Seniority and age difference did not seem to matter to them at all. It was so different from Korea, where younger people had to use honorific terms and bow formally when addressing upperclassmen.

When the waiter brought the bill, I immediately reached for it and offered to pay. "No, no, don't be silly," Ellen said. "We'll go Dutch." I didn't know what she meant by "Dutch" and just stared at her with surprise.

"We'll go Dutch . . . you know, we'll split the bill. Okay, Sookan?"

"Is it all right to do that? I mean, is it all right among good friends?" I asked, feeling rather hurt.

"Sure. It's best that way. We can go out as often as we want without worrying about whose turn it is to pay. All good friends do that here."

"Oh," I said. "I will have to get used to that, too."

"What do you mean?" Ellen asked.

"In Korea, we don't even have such a word as 'Dutch.' One is either the host or the guest. Good friends always take turns treating each other. Each time the bill comes, we all fight over it because we never can remember who paid the time before." I thought fondly of the last time my best friend Bokhi and I had grappled over the bill.

"American style is so much simpler. It's less confusing, and saves time, don't you think?" Ellen smiled proudly. Everything seemed to be easy to her. I could see her point, I suppose, but it felt almost too simple and too practical; it seemed almost cold. I wondered if I would get used to this. I wondered which way was better.

While we were waiting for the bus with the older girls from school, they started talking to me and asking me all about Korea. Everyone was curious about me and where I came from. I was happy to be making friends, and eagerly answered all their questions. As the bus made its way through the busy streets of downtown White Plains, we began to speak of the college dorm rules, the nuns, the professors, and the courses we would like to take.

By the time I got back to school, I had made friends with several sophomores, juniors, and even some seniors. As I was saying goodbye, Ellen yanked me by the arm and said, "Come on, Sookan. Let's get our room set up!"

Chapter Three

The assistant dean recommended that I select a light course load for my first semester. She suggested music appreciation and a studio art class. But I signed up for world literature, world religions, Greek and Roman culture, and early European history. I knew it would be difficult for me, and that I would have to study many more hours than my classmates because of my poor command of English. But armed with what had quickly become my constant companions, my English-Korean and Korean-English dictionaries, I was determined to get through these classes.

My most difficult course was European history, and I always stayed late afterward to copy everything off the board. One morning, as I was busy finishing up my notes, I heard someone say, "Here you are. You'll miss lunch again if you don't hurry." I looked up and saw Marci, who lived in the single room across the hall from Ellen and me.

"Hi, Marci," I said. She smiled timidly back at me. I had caught her staring at me several times over the past few weeks, but each time our eyes met, she would look away. Just the day before, I had run into her on my way back from morning Mass. She had her camera slung over one shoulder, so I said with a smile, "Good morning, Marci. It is a wonderful day for pictures. The sun is so bright today that it makes everything sparkle!" She just nodded, then walked quickly away. I had felt embarrassed and confused. I knew she was a bit shy, but she could have said something to me. Maybe she thought I was silly.

I had watched her walk up the hill with her camera swinging at her side, and thought how wonderful it would be to go for a morning walk and take photos. The campus was so picturesque with the leaves just starting to turn. I wondered if Marci had gotten a picture of the sunrise. I thought of my little camera still tucked away in my suitcase. It was Jaechun's prized possession, yet he had loaded it with film and given it to me, telling me to take some pictures for him as soon as I arrived at school. But there had been no time. I had barely managed to jot a few words on a postcard to tell Mother that I had arrived safely.

"Do you have time for lunch today?" Marci asked. "I saw you in here late yesterday, too."

Still surprised that Marci had stopped by to get me, I answered, "Yes, I always have to stay late to finish my notes. But I think I have everything written down. Okay, let's eat."

Marci was tall and thin, and very pale. Her short,

19

straight brown hair was carelessly tucked behind her ears, and she wore no makeup. Her clothes hung loosely from her thin frame. I thought she was very pretty, though, in a sporty, almost boyish way. She was so different from Ellen.

"Here, let me carry some of those," she said, as she watched me piling my books in my arms. "Don't you want to drop off some of these books? I can take some back to your room for you."

"No, I will need all of them later in the day. I do not have time to walk back to the room. I have class after class, and then I have to do my scholarship work, and afterward, I have to get in as much studying as I can. It takes me a long time to read what they assign. Once I leave my room in the morning, I do not go back until the library closes. And I am *still* behind in my studies!"

As we headed across campus, Ellen, walking with three other girls, spotted us and called out to me. "Long time no see! Come sit with us. I'll save you a seat."

I waved back and smiled. She was right. Though we were roommates, we barely saw each other. I was up and out of the room before Ellen's alarm clock went off, and I usually got back just in time to get ready for lights out. Except for the few words we exchanged in the evening, I only really got to see her if we ran into each other in the dining hall.

"You're so popular, Sookan," Marci said. "I don't know how you manage it all. Do you like it here?"

"Yes, it's exciting to be here, meeting people and

learning so many different things. But it's still difficult for me to express what I am thinking, and it takes me so long to get my reading and studying done. My head hurts by the end of the day. It is hard to think in English all day long, and I know I sound funny."

"You sound just fine. You've adjusted perfectly. I'm the one who looks and sounds awkward all the time." Marci looked down at her feet. "Like yesterday morning when I saw you. I didn't know what to say. Please don't think that I was ignoring you," she said with a pained smile.

"No, do not worry about that," I said, feeling petty for having felt hurt. "I am happy you came to find me today. I think that it's just harder for you to get to know people since you do not have a roommate. Why do you have a single room?"

"Oh, I requested it because I like to read at all hours," she said. "I want to major in classics."

As Marci and I passed The Castle to go to the dining hall, I suddenly remembered that I had to run up to the job placement office on the second floor to see if I could find some extra work. I had checked a couple of times and hadn't found anything. I needed a job on or near campus in order to fit it in with my scholarship work and my class schedule.

"Marci, I'm sorry but I need to see Miss Mullen about something. Would you mind if I meet you at the dining hall later on? Would you please tell Ellen that I will see her later, too?"

"All right," Marci said, looking disappointed. I stood for a minute and watched her round the corner toward the dining hall. How I wished that I had the time to join Marci, to introduce her to Ellen and sit lunching and chatting with them. Unlike Ellen, who was always surrounded by friends, Marci was alone whenever I saw her. I felt sad and frustrated that I didn't have time for her. It must have taken a lot of effort on her part to come and ask me to lunch.

I rushed up the winding marble stairs toward the administration offices. I needed to check in with Miss Mullen, the job placement officer, to see if she had found me a job.

"Oh," Miss Mullen said as I walked through the door, "I was just going to leave a message for you at your dorm, Sookan. Would you be interested in baby-sitting for the Bennetts? Maybe you met Professor Bennett's children, Jimmy and Sarah, during orientation week?"

"No, I was late getting here," I said. "But I am in Professor Bennett's world literature class."

"How could I have forgotten about your brave journey! Sister Reed hasn't stopped talking about how courageous and delightful you are. She is so proud of you."

I blushed, and tears welled up in my eyes. I was relieved to know that Sister Reed thought I was doing all right, and I was grateful to Miss Mullen for telling me so.

"Jane Bennett and I are close friends," she continued. "She and her husband often go into New York City on

the weekends and need a baby-sitter for Jimmy and Sarah. I thought it might suit you to work on weekends
instead of during the week, and they do live right on
campus. They are a lovely family. I really think it will
work out splendidly for everyone."

"Thank you, Miss Mullen. May I know when they
need me?" I felt a bit nervous. Professor Bennett was my
favorite professor, and baby-sitting for his children
seemed rather overwhelming. I thought, *What if the children get bored or don't like me?*

"They need you this Saturday, but I'll have to leave
you a message as to the time."

"Thank you, Miss Mullen," I said again, as I rushed
down the stairs.

On the bench by the door was Marci. "I knew you
would miss lunch," she said. "The cafeteria just closed. I
didn't feel like eating there without you, so I went to the
snack bar and got us two ham sandwiches. Is that okay
with you? And don't worry about Ellen. I stopped by and
told her you couldn't join her today."

I was speechless. All that effort Marci had made for
me!

"Let's go eat our sandwiches. Would you like to see my
favorite spot on campus?" Marci led me down a narrow
path behind The Castle. We climbed a small knoll and
took our places beneath the willow tree there, in the
shade of its cascading branches. We ate our sandwiches
in silence, but smiled broadly at each other. We were

just behind the post office building, but this spot some-how seemed private and distant from the activity of the campus.

I wanted to break the silence and share something with her. "The last time I felt this peaceful," I said, "was when I was with my best friend, Bokhi, in Seoul. It was such a short time ago, but now it seems an eternity away. I wonder how she is. She had been coming over to our house often, not only to see me and my mother, but to see my brother Hyunchun. She has quite a crush on him. Hyunchun is the third oldest of my four brothers. He is tall and handsome, and very outgoing. I think he likes Bokhi, too. He used to just think of her as a little girl, his little sister's friend. But lately, he seems to be realizing what a pretty young woman she is."

"Do you think they'll get married?"

"Oh, I can't tell about those things. It's really up to the older generation. I think my mother would be happy if they married, because she likes Bokhi. But there are a lot of issues to consider. 'Love alone does not make for a good marriage.' " I had heard that adage so often in Korea.

"Do you have brothers and sisters, Marci?" I asked after a pause.

"Just my older sister, Susan. She lives in California with her husband, Bud. I see them once a year when they come back East. But my sister and I are very different. We don't have much to say to each other."

"Oh!" I said, a bit taken aback by her candidness. "I have never spent much time with my sister either. She is a nun, and entered the convent about fifteen years ago, when I was very little. With the wars, there were times when I did not see my sister for a couple years at a time. But lately, we had been going to see her once a month. She is the oldest of the six of us, and we are very proud of her. She teaches and does a lot of work in Seoul for the needy. Her work is very rewarding, she says. Everyone who knows her admires her. Ever since I was little, she has told me that she wants me to work alongside her, and lead a worthy and fulfilling life as she does." I paused, remembering.

"I feel terrible for not writing her. She told me I should keep a journal and write in it every day to reflect on all my new experiences. She wanted me to send her my journal entries once a week instead of writing a separate letter, but I haven't even had a chance to start the journal yet. I know she must be disappointed with me."

"Did you really tell her you would do that? I certainly wouldn't want anyone reading my journal," Marci said, seeming rather confounded.

"Well, she asked me to, and she *is* my older sister. She says she doesn't want us to grow apart; she wants us to share everything. It's just that I am so busy, and there is so much that is new and different around me . . . I can't possibly write everything down every day. I want to obey her, but it's been hard lately."

"Well, you shouldn't feel guilty about it. You are doing so much already. Everyone is amazed at what you are managing as it is."

I was moved by her vehemence. "Oh, thank you, Marci, for saying that. Thank you for the lunch, too. I'm afraid I must get going to my next class now. And I need to stop by the post office to mail another card to my mother."

"I'd better check my mailbox, too, though I doubt anyone will write me. I've lived in Scarsdale all my life and most people I know are a ten-minute drive away."

Marci shrugged her shoulders, then added quickly, "Sookan, I have my car here. Why not come home with me this Saturday? We can study together."

"Oh, Marci, I wish I could, but I have to work this weekend," I said, feeling sorry for myself.

"What kind of work?" Marci asked.

"Baby-sitting. I need to earn some book money," I mumbled, feeling embarrassed about having to talk about money. I didn't like sounding so poor and desperate.

"It'll be fun," Marci said calmly. "And you can come home with me anytime. Come on, let's swing by the post office."

Chapter Four

I stared at the unopened letter from Mother. It felt strange to see my own handwriting on the envelope. The night before I left Seoul, I had stayed up all night attending to last-minute details. One of these was to stamp and address twenty envelopes to myself. Mother did not know English, and I wanted her to feel free to write me without having to ask my brothers to address the envelopes for her. I knew how Mother hated imposing on her children. She always said that young people have their own worries, and that her job was to see that her children had the time to live their own lives.

She was very different from the other mothers I knew. She never talked of filial duty, of the obligations we had to our elders and our ancestors. One of Mother's favorite sayings was "Just as water runs down, so does love." She felt responsible for setting a good example, and just as she loved us, she expected us to love each other, and our children.

She never complained about her hardships, and instead said, "One cannot live looking up. One must look down to those less fortunate and must help them. One has to appreciate what one has in life." With Father gone, she struggled to make ends meet with the little money my brothers were able to earn. And yet, she was always there to help those less fortunate.

This flood of memories overwhelmed me. I longed for my mother. I missed her quiet smile that always seemed to fill me with strength. I felt guilty that I was not by her side. I slowly opened her letter.

Dear Sookan,

It is midnight. Even your ducks are asleep by the pond. They are big now, perhaps a little too big for our small pond. They waddle all around the yard, and sometimes follow me all the way to the street. I can hear your brothers snoring. They fall asleep so quickly; it is the gift of youth.

I am wearing the sweater you insisted on finishing before you left. How stubborn you were to stay up all night before that long trip. But I do love it, and wear it all the time. It keeps me warm on nights like tonight. The cool weather seems to be setting in already, and in the evening, it is quite chilly here. I wonder if we packed enough clothes for you and if you are warm enough in America.

I was in the greenhouse earlier, checking on my chrysanthemums. They will be fluffy and beautiful this season. When they are in full bloom, I will

cut some to give to Father Lee for Sunday
service. My contribution each Sunday is so small
that I thought of supplementing it with my
flowers. It will make me feel that I support my
church.

Your older brothers like to wear the thin cotton
socks you knit before you left. Inchun pulled out
the vest you made, and wore it yesterday. I think
he was glad the weather became cool enough for
it. He looks so handsome in the vest; the light
gray color you chose suits him so well. It was a
good thing you learned how to knit as that is one
of the things I never learned.

We all miss you. The house feels empty
without you.

I read your postcards as soon as our good
mailman brings them. He is getting old now, and
has been having more and more trouble with his
legs this year. But he knows how important your
letters are, and always brings them all the way up
to the house for me. I am so grateful to him that
I offer him a cup of tea every time he comes. He
asked me to say hello to you for him.

In the evening, when we are all together, we
read your postcards aloud. I am sorry we are not
sending you any money. What little you had with
you must have been gone long ago. I think your
brothers do not write because they have no
money to send you. Forgive this helpless mother

who sends her daughter so far away and cannot even mail a little pocket money each month.

I am glad you like your new friends and college in America. It must be hard to adjust to the new culture and the new way of doing things. The language alone must cause you problems. Although you sound so cheerful and happy, I can imagine the difficulties you face. I will never know exactly what they are, though. I know you do not tell me things because you don't want to worry me.

I know you will blossom there, though things may be difficult for you now. It is always hard to be away from your homeland. The first year is always the worst, I think. We are all fine. Don't worry about anything here. And please make sure to get enough sleep.

You will see that four years will zoom by. Before you know it, we will be talking face to face.

Your loving mother

I felt melancholy after reading Mother's letter. Despite her reassurances, I could tell that things were difficult back home. I pictured her worried expression, and my brothers' somber faces. I was glad that I had never mentioned anything about my scholarship work in the dining hall, my need to work for pocket money, and my late nights finishing my school work. I was ashamed at not being there to help Mother through her hardships. I knew how much she had always missed my sister, her firstborn, and how she must miss me. Now, she had no daughters at home.

Through her letter, I felt her love and concern for me. But what comforted me most was her deep faith and trust. She was sure I would succeed in America, and would come back to her.

Wiping away the tears that had filled my eyes, I opened my books and began to study. *I must do well on my history test tomorrow. I must make Mother proud of me.*

Chapter Five

It was a quiet Saturday morning. All the other girls in the dorm were still fast asleep, recovering from the excitement of the mixer the night before. Marci had left Friday afternoon to go home to Scarsdale. I wished I could have joined her; she looked lonesome. Ellen had popped into our room after the mixer, staying just long enough to chastise me for not attending. I tried to explain how far behind I was on my reading, and how early I had to get up on Saturday to baby-sit, but she said, "You just have to make time for it. It's important." Then she kissed me goodbye and left for Princeton to spend the weekend with Kyle.

With my book bag slung over my shoulder, I made my way through the dense early morning fog and headed to the far end of campus where the Bennetts lived. I had promised to be there by eight to baby-sit. The sun struggled futilely to penetrate the haze, and the damp winds sent a shiver through me. It was only mid-October, but the air was chilly. I buttoned my light sweater and ran.

I was apprehensive about the day ahead of me. I had

baby-sat often in Korea, but I wondered if I could handle the task in America, speaking English. To make matters worse, these were the children of my professor. *What if they don't like me? What if I can't keep them entertained or if they are naughty?* I ran faster to rid myself of these nagging doubts.

I came across a little brook, and bent down to pick out one of the shiny pebbles from the stream. I dried it, warmed it in my hands, then put it deep in my pocket. I wanted to keep a bit of nature with me. Small river stones somehow comforted me. They seemed so peaceful and carefree, glittering and dancing with the undulations of the cool, clear water. I would have loved to sit and listen to the stream while waiting for the sun to conquer the fog and shine through the leaves of the tall trees. I loved this part of campus, and regretted that I did not usually have time to walk and rest here.

When I knocked on the Bennetts' door, I heard the sound of four feet charging toward it. A boy with short brown hair and a girl with long brown curls flung open the door. They stared at me shyly as they tried to catch their breath. Then the boy bellowed, "Mom! Mom!"

"Hello," I said as I entered the house. "My name is Sookan. And you are Jimmy and Sarah, right?" I was relieved that I had remembered their names.

A frail-looking woman dashed out of a back room and said, "You must be Sookan. Miss Mullen speaks so highly of you. I'm glad you have the time to baby-sit. Professor Bennett and I have to go into the city this morning, but we should be back by three. I see you already met Jimmy and Sarah. Children, did you say hello to Sookan?"

"Hello," they said in unison, before running toward the kitchen and shouting, "Dad, Dad, your student is here!"

"Great! Bring her over here into the kitchen. We can all have breakfast together before Mom and I leave." His familiar voice rang through the house.

Sarah and Jimmy rushed back and, staring at me as if I might vanish, escorted me to the kitchen without a word. They both studied my every step.

Hesitantly I asked, "How old are you, Jimmy?"

"Six and three-quarters."

"And you, Sarah?"

"Five. But I can do almost everything Jimmy can," she said, poking her brother in the ribs.

Jimmy seemed annoyed at this presumptuous remark, and raced ahead of us into the kitchen. Standing at the stove was Professor Bennett wearing a large red apron that said "Best Chef" in bold black letters. He waved us in with his spatula, and said, "Sookan, come on in. You can sample my cooking."

I could hardly believe my eyes! Never before had I seen a man cook or even enter a kitchen. Cooking was a woman's job. Mother was always in the kitchen alone, except when I kept her company. At mealtime, she and I always did the serving, and afterward, we always cleaned up. My brothers just sat at the table, and talked and laughed and ate.

Though tired and flushed from cooking, Mother never seemed happier than when she watched her sons gobble up all the food she had spent the day preparing. She would busily run back and forth between the living room and the kitchen to make sure they had as much as they wanted. I, on the other hand, derived no joy from this task. I knew I was doing my duty as a daughter and sister, but I resented the fact that it was always Mother and me who had to do all the work. *Wouldn't it be wonderful if the men would serve us sometime?* I used to think to myself, knowing all too well that this was a fantasy. But now, right before me, was my very own professor slaving over his family's scrambled eggs. It seemed like a miracle to me.

I stood watching Professor Bennett as he turned over the bacon, then instinctively pivoted to catch the toast as it popped from the toaster. He skillfully buttered the bread and placed it before his children.

Mrs. Bennett appeared from upstairs and said, "Soo-kan, why are you still standing? Please, have a seat."

"Oh, I thought I should wait until you and Professor Bennett sat down," I said. It was rude to seat oneself before one's elders. And besides, I was too shocked at the sight of a man cooking to even think of sitting.

"Sookan, please sit down. Make yourself at home. Walt will serve us this morning. Every Saturday and

Sunday, he gives me a break from kitchen duty." She smiled affectionately at her husband.

As we sat and ate, I confessed how surprised I was to see a man working in the kitchen, and how different things were in Korea.

Professor Bennett just smiled and said, "It's amazing how well you are doing in this strange land, Sookan, and how quickly you've adapted. It's hard to believe you have been here less than two months. Sarah, Jimmy, don't tire her out too much today." I blushed at his kind remarks.

The professor did the dishes while his wife finished getting dressed. The children and I stayed in the kitchen and helped him. How wonderful to all be in the kitchen, talking and cleaning up together. I kept thinking of my poor mother, who would never have such an experience.

After Professor and Mrs. Bennett left, Sarah brought out her favorite book, *Madeline,* and asked me to read it to her. Jimmy had taken out his train and was racing the wheels with his hand. The house was abuzz with the sound of the whizzing train.

As I read to Sarah about the twelve little girls who ate, brushed their teeth, and slept in two straight lines at their French convent school, Jimmy looked over my shoulder and began correcting my pronunciation. It must have been awful for them to hear the way I mispronounced things. Each time Jimmy corrected me, I reread the words and tried to imitate his pronunciation and intonation. He seemed pleased when my words sounded like his. Sometimes he made me repeat a phrase two or even three times. I followed his instruction and we made our way through *Madeline*. To my surprise, Sarah did not complain once. By the time we finished the book, Jimmy was seated by my side; he seemed delighted to be my teacher, and I appreciated his help. Only a child would correct every little sound and syllable so honestly and enthusiastically. I thanked Jimmy for correcting me, and he turned bright red, then disappeared into his room.

Sarah, who had been watching me intently as I read, said, "Your eyes are so black and tiny. Let's have an eye fight." She got up, stood directly in front of me, and began steadfastly glaring at me. I knew this game. We played it in Korea, too. I sat and stared back into her big brown eyes, and I tried not to blink. She was so serious, and wore such a stern expression for a little girl that I broke into laughter.

Sarah clapped with glee and said, "See, your eyes are too small to win the eye fight."

"No, no. It's not because they are small. It's because my eyes are tired from reading so many books and not going to sleep early enough," I said, feeling weary all of a sudden.

"Then close your eyes and sleep, and I'll comb your black hair. All my dolls have blond hair. Can I comb yours?"

I nodded, closed my eyes, and rested my head on the sofa, letting my hair fall over the back of it. Sarah's plastic comb soon got tangled up in my thick hair, and she tenaciously yanked and yanked to get it free. I tried to rest my eyes and let her play. I could hear Jimmy enjoying his electric train in the next room. After a while, I felt something sharp digging into my scalp. "Oh, Sarah, that hurts!"

"Look, I fixed your hair with pins and ribbons," she said with delight as she handed me a mirror. I had to laugh. She had made me look like a cartoon character from outer space. My hair was standing up in all directions, and was adorned with ribbons of every color.

She then began removing the pins, pulling my hair along with them. I heard myself scream, and Jimmy immediately ran over to us. "Sarah, I'm going to tell Daddy that you were mean to his student," he threatened. To me, he said, "You are too nice. Nobody lets her play with real hair. Not even Mommy."

Sarah pouted, and glared at Jimmy. I was sorry I had let out a scream and said, "Oh, it's all right, Jimmy. I said she could play with my hair. We will stop for now, though. Okay, Sarah?"

Then, to make Sarah laugh, I picked up her little hand and said, "Look how cute and small your hands are compared to my big ones!" I remembered how this used to amuse me when I was young.

Sarah put her hand against mine and we stretched our fingers as much as we could. I noticed how light and pink her skin was against mine. "I think God ran out of pink paint when he was making me, and used the yellow paint he had left over."

"No," she retorted, "that's not why. He is God. If he

wanted to, he could have made more pink paint. He *wanted* to use yellow paint for your hand. It makes you special!"

Jimmy looked over at us and clearly thought this was ludicrous prattle. He made a face at his chatty little sister, and went back to racing his train around the living room.

When we finished lunch, the phone rang. It was Mrs. Bennett. She and her husband couldn't be back at three as they had planned. She asked me if I might stay with the children until the evening. She would drive me back to the dorm when they returned.

I, of course, said yes, but was concerned. I had so much studying to do, and I had promised myself that I would write a letter to my sister. I had already let too much time pass without writing to her, and I knew I was disappointing her.

Suddenly, I realized that Sarah and Jimmy were staring at me and looking worried. I smiled and said, "What would you like to do? Your parents will be late, but everything is okay."

"Oh, goodie. We can play some more," said Sarah. "Let's take a walk to the millhouse."

"Yeah, we can look for garden snakes," added Jimmy.

"Yuck! They're all hibernating anyway," said Sarah, as she stuck her tongue out at her brother.

We took a walk to the old stone millhouse, and peeked inside. The roof had blown off long ago, and all that stood were the walls. Tall grass was growing inside, and the building smelled damp and earthy. It looked like one of the old Roman ruins in my textbooks. We kept walking alongside the stream. Jimmy watched for garden snakes, while Sarah held my hand and helped me pick wildflowers. I felt comfortable with the two of them and decided not to think about school or anything else that I had to do.

We went back to the house, and played for the rest of the afternoon. I drew flowers and trees with Sarah, and snakes and bugs with Jimmy, and we made all sorts of cut-out decorations. It had been a happy, exhausting day for all of us.

After supper, the children finally got to sleep, and I tried to read the books I had brought with me. But my mind wandered. I thought of how much I had enjoyed playing with the children, and it made me uneasy to know that I was going to be paid for being with them. In Korea, we never got paid for watching the neighbors' children. It was just something we did without a second thought.

My schoolbag was bulging with books that needed to be read. But I wanted to do something special for the Bennetts. I looked around the house for ideas. I had already tidied up all the rooms. Then, I saw what I was looking for.

In the far corner of the house was a small greenhouse. Inside, the plants seemed terribly neglected. Dead leaves hung limply from some. Others seemed to be growing lopsided with abandon. Several were completely dead.

Empty clay pots, bags of soil, and gardening tools cluttered the corners.

Before I started to work on the greenhouse, I went back to check on Jimmy and Sarah. They were both asleep, but I left their doors ajar so that I would be able to hear them if they woke. Then, I returned to the greenhouse, began to pick all the brown leaves off, cut the dead stems, and tie sticks to some of the plants to get them to stand straight. I watered everything, wiped down the leaves of each plant, transplanted some overgrown jade plants to bigger pots, and tidied up the room. I gathered all the cactuses on one side, placed all the African violets in front of the window, and put the big jade plants in the center. I had often watched Mother work in her greenhouse, so I felt comfortable here.

When I looked at my watch, I realized I had been in the greenhouse for several hours. I looked at my work, and was pleased. But suddenly, I began to worry that the professor and his wife might not have wanted me to touch their greenhouse. It hadn't even occurred to me before. When I saw the neglected garden, I just instinctively wanted to take care of the plants. I would have to tell them, and apologize for just plunging ahead without even asking. I would tell them as soon as they got home. I stood by the window, watching for their car, but after a while, decided to sit down and read.

Mrs. Bennett gently woke me at midnight and said that her husband would drive me home. I had missed curfew, but the professor would explain it to Sister Casey at Mass the next day. I grabbed my things together and rushed to the car.

The following Monday, when I returned to my dorm from the library, the receptionist at the front desk pointed to a long white box tied with a red velvet ribbon.

"Sookan, that's for you. It came this afternoon."

The box was marked "Valerie Florist." I said I would be back to get it after I dropped off my books. As I was heading up the stairs to my room, I ran into Ellen.

"Oh, Sookan, I was coming down to pick up your flowers. I wanted you to see the box waiting for you at reception, but they've been there all afternoon, and I was just about to give up on you. Wait here, and I'll get them and we can walk upstairs together."

Ellen beamed as she put the box down on my bed.

"Open them up! Let's see who they're from! Do you have an admirer that I don't know about?"

Marci, who must have heard Ellen and me talking as we walked down the corridor, poked her head into our room, and said, "What's this?"

When I untied the velvet bow and lifted off the top, I saw an enormous bunch of roses, white lilies, tiger lilies, tiny orchids, red and white carnations, and fluffy white chrysanthemums. They were beautiful and made the whole room smell of spring. Ellen immediately hunted for the little white envelope and said, "Hurry, read it."

The note said: "What a grand surprise to see our ne-glected greenhouse transformed into a lovely little garden. It seems that a special elf was at work. Thanks for everything on Saturday. The children learned so much from you and had so much fun. You must be a natural born teacher. They adore you and chose these flowers themselves. Hope you will have time to come again. Love, Jane."

A check was also enclosed for Saturday. Ellen looked disappointed that the flowers were from the Bennetts, but Marci was delighted and looked at me proudly. She then shook her head at Ellen, and ran out to the hall closet, shouting, "Let me see if I can find a big vase."

She came back with three small vases. "These won't do for those tall flowers," she said, looking disappointed.

"Oh, they'll be fine. I can use them all," I said. I made three arrangements and gave one to Marci for her room, one to Ellen for her dresser, and kept one for my desk.

As usual, the "lights out" bell rang all too quickly. Marci headed back to her room across the hallway, calling, "Good night."

"In the future, I expect you to receive flowers and chocolates from boys you meet at the Friday mixers," said Ellen, wagging her manicured index finger at me with a stern look.

I smiled and said, "Maybe I *will* show up at one of the mixers and surprise you. Good night, Ellen, and thanks for bringing up the flowers and always thinking of me." I drew in a deep breath of the deliciously fragrant air, picturing my stroll along the stream with Sarah and Jimmy.

Chapter Six

It was quarter to five, and I was rushing to make it over to the dining hall. This semester, for scholarship work, I had been assigned to waitress the dinner shift from five to eight Sunday through Thursday. On these evenings, our school had formal, candle-lit dinners with a strict dress code. All the girls were required to wear dresses, high heels, and gloves.

I darted into the little locker room that was reserved for the kitchen staff, and changed into my uniform, a white starched blouse, black straight skirt, and low patent leather pumps. As I tore into the dining hall to sign in, Peggy Stone said, "Sookan, you can slow down. You're the first one here again." Peggy was a senior and the captain of the thirteen waitresses. She asked me to begin setting the tables and to place candles on each one.

Promptly, at ten minutes to six, we were told to light the candles. I loved this part of the evening, when the wicks sizzled in defiance before taking flame, then filled the room with the smell of warm wax. As usual, when all the candles were lit, I stood by Peggy as she dimmed the big chandelier. Though we did this day after day, it was always a wondrous moment for me. The dining hall was suddenly transformed into a magical place, warmed by the dancing pools of flickering candlelight. I embraced this peaceful moment in my otherwise hectic day.

Through the picture window, I could see the students walking toward the candle-lit room. They all looked so elegant in their high heels and gloves. I pictured myself all dressed up, walking with them in a leisurely way, and chatting about the last mixer. But I could not daydream long, for it was time to pick up my tray to begin serving.

I was assigned to serve the four tables near the front of the dining room. Fortunately, my section was nearest the kitchen counter, and I didn't have to carry the heavy serving platters far. Ellen always tried to sit at one of my tables, and once in a while, we could share a few words or a quick glance as I rushed back and forth.

"Sookan," Ellen said as she entered, "why don't you try to leave the library a bit early tonight or wake me up tomorrow morning before you tiptoe out of the room?"

"All right. Why? Anything special happening?" I asked as I motioned for her and her friends to sit down.

"Well, I miss talking to you! That's all." Ellen smiled as she carefully eased off her white gloves. I hurried back to the kitchen to pick up the appetizers.

Later that evening, after clearing the tables and sweeping the floor, I signed out and began the slow walk back to the library. Once the students left, I always ran around as fast as I could hoping to finish up early and have a little more time to study. But I was always so tired afterward; my legs felt wobbly, and my arms and back ached.

That evening, instead of walking across the lawn, I took a shortcut through The Castle. As I was passing through the dimly lit corridors, I saw Marci hunched over a book in a corner chair. She had on a comfortable sweater, her blue wool pants, and penny loafers. Marci never came to dinner in the dining hall. She had once told me she thought the dress code and the formality were "ridiculously pretentious" and a waste of time. She ate at the snack bar, where the senior scholarship students made delicious hamburgers, sandwiches, and french fries until all hours of the night. It was strange to find her here.

"I thought you might come this way," she said. "We haven't seen much of each other lately."

I felt a lump in my throat. How wonderful she was to go out of her way for me. With my schedule, I never had a chance to spend time with my friends.

Together, we headed toward the library, stopping at the post office on our way.

Outside, I paused, wobbling slightly on my weary legs. "Marci, look! It's so clear tonight you can see all the stars."

"Sookan, are you okay? You look so pale and tired."

"Oh, I'll be fine. It's just that there is so much running around in the dining hall. I can't wait to be a sophomore; then, I can do my scholarship duty in the library."

Marci smiled awkwardly and said nothing.

46

"It's not so bad, really. It gives me a chance to meet other scholarship students. We get to talk a bit while we set up. And I do love that room when all the candles are lit." Suddenly I couldn't stop talking. "I love watching the patterns the candlelight casts on the ceiling and walls. Those few minutes before all the students come in fill me with such a feeling of peace and happiness. It's hard to explain, but those moments carry me through the evening. At night, when I return to the library and am feeling angry about not having enough time to study, I think of the dancing candlelight and it makes me smile. I wish you would come early one day and see it with me." Then, I felt silly for chattering about candles for so long, and quickly opened the door to the post office.

Waiting for me was a letter from my sister and a note from Miss Mullen in the job placement office. I opened the note first, which said, "The local Girl Scouts club would like you to speak about Korea this Saturday at noon. If you could wear your native outfit, it would be a great treat for them. Let me know."

I was glad to hear from Miss Mullen, but I was worried about not having enough time for all of my work.

"What is it?" asked Marci, who must have noticed that I was upset. I handed her the note.

"Sookan, if you don't want to, you should just say so," Marci said, after reading the note.

Taking a deep breath, I said, "No, I should do it. I am the only Korean here and if I say no, there is nobody else who can talk about Korea to the little girls."

"Yeah, but if it's too much, you just can't. Miss Mullen of all people will understand. She knows how many jobs you work."

"I know. But I feel that I should do these things. I understand that I am a foreigner and look different, and that people are curious about me. It is my duty to help people understand me, and my culture. And I like meeting new people. I think I would really enjoy meeting the Girl Scouts." I sighed. "It just gets so hard after a while. I keep falling further and further behind in my studies, and I'm beginning to worry that I might actually fail some of my courses. And I'm sometimes tired of this feeling that I always have to explain myself. I have to work for every little bit of acceptance and understanding. Sometimes I wish I could get lost in the crowd, and just go about my business. That's why I don't really like wearing my *hanbok*. It makes me feel so different and so all alone. It must be a comfort to be like everyone else. There's so much pressure when you're different."

Marci was deep in thought, and I wondered if she had even been listening to me. It was silly of me to go on and on. Maybe it was too hard for Marci to relate to what I was saying. After all, she had grown up fifteen minutes away from here.

"I think I know how you feel," Marci said, to my surprise. "I might look like everyone else, but I feel out of place here. I'm out of place even in my own home. I feel like an oddball wherever I am."

I didn't know how to respond. I knew Marci was shy

and still trying to settle in at school, but I was surprised by her words.

"My parents and my sister are so much alike," she continued. "My parents adore her. Dad and Susan are always talking about photography together, and Susan and my mom are always shopping or going to the beauty parlor together. She is everything they hoped for in a child. She's outgoing, popular, and beautiful. I know that when they look at me, they wonder where they went wrong, and why I didn't turn out more like Susan." Marci looked down at her feet while she talked. "Every once in a while, I try to fit in and be what my parents want me to be. I keep trying to develop an interest in photography, but I can't. It's just not who I am. My father actually wants me to take over his chemical company someday! I can't think of anything I would like less. It's a waste of time for me to pretend to like things just to please them; I refuse to do that anymore. I know what I want for my life. I want to be a classics professor."

Although Marci spoke matter-of-factly, I was amazed at how strong and clear-minded she was. I could never say such things. I even felt bad when I thought those thoughts. In Korea, you must do what is expected of you and live up to your responsibilities. It is so important not to let your elders down. I was shocked to hear Marci say these things, but strangely invigorated.

I didn't know what to say to her, so I just stared silently at the letter in my hand. It was the first piece of mail from my sister. My heart started to pound. I was afraid to open it. I knew I had disobeyed her by not writing, and I feared her letter would be an angry one.

Looking at the envelope, Marci said, "Hmm, a letter from home."

"It's from my sister. I still haven't written her," I replied sheepishly.

"Well, you probably want to read it. I think I'll head back to the dorm, anyway. I'll see you later, okay?"

Nodding my head with an anxious smile, I said, "Thanks, Marci. Thanks for waiting for me. See you later!"

I sat down in a corner of the post office and carefully opened Theresa's letter.

My dear little sister Sookan,

Tonight, in the peace of my room, I have decided to write you because you are my loving sister and you have been in my thoughts constantly since your last visit to the convent. I have much other work to do, but you are important to me.

It was another crazy day. My work at the hospital and the school is difficult, and often, very sad. It has been over a year since the war ended, and still, so many people are in need of so many basics. I cannot wait for you to return and join me in my work. We can do much good together. It is a noble life to help others. As a nun, you can do so much more for the needy, without the obligations and impediments that married life places on you. Why be a slave to a man? Why fill your days washing his socks and making his dinner? You can be helping people who truly need you.

As I have said many times before, you must not forget those less fortunate. I have not heard from you yet, and wonder about your life in America. Remember, you should be keeping a journal each day; it is important for your spiritual growth to find some quiet time at the end of each day for reflection and prayer. Simply send your journal entries to me once a week. I will keep them for you and give them to you when you return. This way, I can know what your life is like, and we two sisters can share everything. We can share all our thoughts and feelings, as well as a mutual objective. I still have no idea as to what your first day was like. How can we be close and be of one heart and mind if I do not receive a letter from you? It is already the end of October, and not a single piece of correspondence from you. I hope and pray you do not lose sight of our goal. I pray that you will not allow yourself to be swept away by American culture and all the things you see in such a rich country.

Judging from your hurried postcards to Mother, it sounds like you are having a wonderful time with your new friends. How difficult could it be to find a few moments to send me a letter? Please write and share your life with me so that we will not grow apart during these four long years.

You are always in my prayers.

Your loving sister, Theresa

I folded the thin airmail sheets and put them back in the envelope. I thought of my high school days, when I had faithfully visited my sister on the first Sunday of each month, the only time visitors were allowed. In the quiet, sunny sitting room, she would ask me about everything that happened at school and at home, and about everything going on in the neighborhood. She would speak of her calling and her work. She spoke with such feeling and conviction. I looked up to her. Everyone did. I listened to all the plans she had made for me. She spoke about how we would work side by side helping many people, comforting those in despair, and teaching young children. It all sounded fine then.

But now, as I read her letter, she sounded very different to me. It was as if I had never known her. Her tone was so much less kind than Mother's. I wondered if my sister still loved me. She didn't seem to understand the difficulties of facing a new culture and language. Didn't she realize that I might be struggling to settle into college life and to keep pace in my classes? Mother understood without my ever saying a word.

I didn't know what to think. Perhaps Theresa was right to be angry with me. She had asked me to tell her everything about my new life, and I had disobeyed her. I had neglected my duties as a younger sister. Perhaps I was being selfish, always busy with my own life and ignoring her wishes and needs. Was I becoming shallow? How could I be a good person when I had disappointed my own sister? Maybe I should have been honest about my struggles. But I hadn't wanted to worry Mother. I felt like such a failure.

How foolish I had been even to think of stopping by a Friday mixer! I didn't have time for such things. My sister would be very disappointed to know that I was wasting my time in that way. I heard the dorm bell sound and realized I had been sitting in the post office for quite a while. Wiping my tears away, I quickly gathered my books and rose from the hard bench.

Chapter Seven

From the large library window, I looked out at the maple tree, trembling against the gusts of November wind and surrendering its dry, brown leaves. Fall was almost over and I hadn't had a chance to take even one photo of the beautiful foliage.

It was late. I gathered my books and headed toward the dorm, looking forward to hearing Ellen's cheerful voice. Blanketed in the shadow of trees, the brightly lit dorm was like a beacon. I rubbed my tired eyes. The endless hours of studying, the scholarship work, the responsibilities of being the only Korean student, and my worries over disappointing my family all overwhelmed me. I still had not answered my sister's letter, but her voice rang in my ears.

When I rounded the corner toward my room, I saw Ellen in her powder pink bathrobe, satin slippers, and head of pink curlers, standing in the hallway saying good-bye to some friends. As soon as she spotted me, she rushed over. "Hi, stranger. Give me some of those books; I can't even see your face! You know, you're so rarely here that Kyle is beginning to think I've made you up. Why don't you come to this Friday's mixer and then come home with me for the weekend? Princeton is playing Dartmouth, and Kyle invited both of us. He wants you to meet his roommate, too. Princeton is only fifteen minutes away from my home, you know." She excitedly said all of this in one breath.

"Oh, Ellen, thank you. I wish I could!" Ellen made it sound like so much fun, and like such an important aspect of college life. I wondered what it would be like to go to a mixer or to a football game. What was I missing?

"Why not this time?" Ellen said, knitting her brows.

"Well, some visitors from Europe are coming this weekend and the international student office asked me to show them around the campus. And I am more behind than ever on my reading."

"Last time I asked you to come home with me, you had to speak to the Ladies Garden Club! You're a college student and need to enjoy college life. You're not a diplomat, you know. That's what my mother says each time I tell her why you can't come visit. I feel like marching up to Miss Mullen and telling her that you simply don't have time to do all these things."

With a sigh, I said, "As a foreign scholarship student, it is my obligation to help out with these international activities. But I wish I didn't have to do so many of them."

"It's all those extra things that are keeping you from enjoying the real college experience," Ellen said. "It's important for you to check out the social scene. You should come to a mixer, and spend an evening playing bridge at the snack bar. Everyone is always asking for you. I'm *serious*; these are important parts of college life."

"I know. But it will have to be this way for now. Next year, you'll see, I will take everyone up on all these rain checks I have been accumulating."

"Well, you promised to spend Thanksgiving with me, remember?" Ellen said. "You said yes your first day here."

"I remember. I'm looking forward to it," I said, thinking back to the day I met Ellen.

"I guess you and Kyle will have to wait till Thanksgiving dinner to meet each other. My parents said I could invite him since he won't be going home to Madison," Ellen said, looking pleased at the thought of getting everyone together.

"You know, Ellen, I did see Kyle once." I reddened as I thought of the day I had watched the two of them together.

"When?" Ellen asked.

"Last weekend. I was looking out the library window when I saw you sitting under a tree with Kyle. He was lying down, resting his head on your lap."

"Well, what did you think?" she asked.

"Oh, he is very handsome, and he is so tall! I could tell when you walked down the hill together. I thought it was sweet the way he bent down and kissed you. It was like a scene out of the movies."

"You mean you saw us and never said a word to me?" Ellen said, wide-eyed.

"Well, whenever I saw you, you always had something exciting to report. Besides, I needed some time to think about it all."

"To think about what?"

"Everything is so different here," I said slowly. "In Korea, such a thing would not be possible. Even married couples do not show such affection in public. There is no hand holding, no kissing, and no resting under trees together. But what is shameful in Korea seems accepted and natural here. Sometimes the differences are so mind-boggling that I need to give myself time to get used to the new ways of thinking. But it's funny," I mused. "In many ways I feel so comfortable here — sometimes even more comfortable than I felt at home."

"What do you mean, Sookan?" asked Ellen.

"Well, for one thing, I feel the same warmth and closeness toward you and Marci that I do toward some friends I have known for years at home. I come from so far away and look so different from you that I am some-times surprised at how at ease I feel with you and Mar-ci — and it has only been a few months. Isn't it strange? I think it is because your culture encourages people to speak openly and frankly." I looked at Ellen helplessly. I was not sure if I had made any sense to her, because I myself was not completely sure of why I felt so much at home in such a new and different environment.

"Friendships are special," Ellen said. "Friendships can cut through a lot. Are you sure you can't make some excuse and come home with me for the weekend?"

"I'm sorry, Ellen. I can't. But you'll have a great time with Kyle." Then I asked, "Don't your parents mind that you spend so much time with him when you go home for the weekend?"

"Of course, they wish I would spend more time with them, but they actually don't know much about Kyle yet. I tell them that I go to Princeton to visit my cousin and go out with his friends, one of whom is Kyle. I'm an only child, and I know it will be hard for them to accept that Kyle and I are so serious. But soon I'll tell them, and they will just have to get used to the idea. Kyle and I are in love; we are meant for each other. He is the man I will marry." She spoke with such conviction. "I am eighteen years old, after all. I have to lead my own life."

I was too startled to respond. I was amazed at her independence and her ability to decipher so lucidly what was important to her. She was in charge of her own life. This would be unthinkable in Korea, where the happiness of both families was more important than the happiness of the couple themselves. Young girls' lives were tied to the family. Love was not the determining factor. But seeing Ellen so happy and so madly in love with Kyle, I began to wonder if she were not right.

"Sookan, I've been wanting to ask you something. I know it's a chore for you, but would you wear your beautiful *hanbok* for Thanksgiving? I'll help you iron it and get dressed and everything. Would you mind terribly? It's so pretty," Ellen rambled, "and I want to show you off."

"I have a better idea, Ellen. *You* can wear it. We'll surprise your parents and Kyle!"

"Can I? Do you think I'll look good in it?" Ellen asked rhapsodically.

"You'll look beautiful. You can wear the winter *hanbok,* the deep blue one."

The bell rang for lights out. I got ready for bed in a hurry, and shut off the lights.

"Sookan? Have you ever kissed a boy?" Ellen asked, tucking herself in her bed.

"No."

"Hugged one?"

"No," I said, embarrassed and annoyed.

"Don't you ever want to fall in love, get married, and have a family? Are you really planning to be a nun like your sister?"

"I've always just assumed I would be a nun," I said. "Ever since I can remember, my sister has told me of all the things we would do together as nuns. It sounded fine before, but lately I'm not sure. My sister does find her work fulfilling; she teaches children, and she helps so many people. I think I would like to do that, too."

"But Sookan, you can be married *and* do all of that! You can be married, have a family, and still be a teacher, or a social worker, or a volunteer if you want. You don't have to be a nun to help people!" Ellen continued to talk as I drifted off to sleep.

Chapter Eight

The assembly hall was packed and bustling. It was freshman election week, and there were many committees to be chosen: the student council, the student-faculty liaison committee, the dance committee, and others. For the past several days, Ellen had been lobbying to chair the dance committee, and her bridge buddies were all campaigning for her. As Marci and I walked into the hall, we saw Ellen behind the refreshment table, pouring hot beverages, handing out cookies, and chatting with everyone.

Marci and I took seats in the back. Marci had brought two books, *Agamemnon* and *The Last Days of Socrates*. She had no interest in school elections, and immediately immersed herself in her reading. No one was excused from this daylong meeting; we all had to participate in the election process. Many girls had brought their knitting.

I had my airmail stationery with me and hoped I would have a chance to write to my sister. Her words haunted me. I couldn't bear knowing that she disapproved of me.

I would write her a long letter and fill her in on some of the things that I had been doing.

The nomination process began. Ellen, nominated for the dance committee, walked to the stage to make her speech. Her voice, which often sounded shrill in the hallways of the dorm, was forceful and resonant in the assembly hall. Ellen accepted the nomination, and told us that she was very well qualified for the position, having run many dances at her high school. She reminded everyone that she had attended every single Friday night mixer so far, and had helped organize the refreshments each time. She wrapped up her speech with many new ideas, such as a winter ball and a spring swing dance, which she would organize if elected. The applause welled forth. After that enthusiastic speech, no one doubted that she was the best-qualified person among us to chair the committee. I became so caught up in the excitement of the nomination process that I listened to every speech, and even forgot to drink my hot chocolate.

Nominations for student council were next.

"Sookan Bak," they called. I was stunned. I could not believe someone had nominated me. My heart started to pound. I wanted to accept the nomination. I would have loved to serve on the student council, and I was sure I could do a good job.

But when it was my turn to make a speech, I heard myself saying, "Thank you for nominating me. But I cannot accept."

One of the girls sitting in front of me turned around and said, "Sookan, why not?"

Another girl said, "You have a good chance. We will vote for you."

I thanked them, but said, "It's the time. I just can't manage another thing. As it is, I can barely pass my courses."

I thought it had been Ellen who had nominated me, but I heard her explaining, "She is already so busy. I know she just doesn't have the time. That's why."

I looked at Marci. She was busy taking notes on her reading, oblivious to what went on around her. I knew she had not been the one, either.

They moved on with the proceedings. I was still surprised that my name had been called. I had hardly been able to get to know my classmates because I was always busy running from one thing to another. It made me happy to know they liked me enough to nominate me, and I was deeply sorry that I hadn't been able to accept.

After I declined, I sat, slumped and disappointed, in my seat. I was tired of always feeling so overwhelmed, so harried. Why was I not like every other college student, just worrying about my studies?

I looked blankly down at the untouched stationery on my lap. I had to write to Theresa today. I got up, and headed to the little lounge next to the assembly hall. There, I started to write.

My dear elder sister,

I received your letter and deeply apologize for not having written, as you had asked. Although everyone at home is always on my mind, my college schedule does not leave me much time for writing letters. I will do my best in the future.

A few weekends ago, I was at my English professor's house, and he cooked breakfast for his children and his wife and me. It was wonderful to see a man cooking for his family. The whole family was together in the kitchen, talking and setting the table while he worked. I thought how nice it would be for Mother to have our brothers keep her company in the kitchen and maybe even try cooking. I wish such things were possible in Korea. I know our brothers help in many other ways, but it was surprising and so nice to see a man in the kitchen. And he was a good cook, too. I just thought I would share this with you because you said you wanted to know everything I see and do here. America is so very different.

Another thing I have marveled at is the open communication between different age groups. Freshmen can talk to seniors about all sorts of things. They can be good friends, and go places together. The distinction in rank and age is not so rigid as in Korea. It is not that people are impolite here. It is just that everyone is friendly to each other, regardless of status.

Today is election day at the college. I have enjoyed seeing my friends stand up on stage to give their campaign speeches. They talk about themselves and their accomplishments, and why they are qualified for the position. It is such a contrast to Korea, where a woman would never think of expressing herself. Here, the nuns encourage all the girls to speak for themselves. They encourage us to study hard, but also to be sociable, to learn to mingle with other college students, both male and female.

Here, they do not place so much emphasis on patience, humility, family harmony, and silence as we do in Korea. It is a much more open, equal, and individualistic society. Americans' different attitudes and ways of viewing things make it difficult for me to continue to act the way I did in Korea. I try to follow your advice as much as I can, but I often have to modify my actions and even my way of thinking in order to fit in here.

Although the culture is so foreign to me, I have not had trouble making friends. At first, most of the girls were very curious about me and my life in Korea. They asked what we eat, what kinds of beds we sleep in, if we use chopsticks, if we sit on the floor, what religions we practice

. . . But after the initial barrage of questions, it all became very relaxed.

Everything is still so new, and for now, I am busy trying to learn and adapt as quickly as I can. But it is strange, for although there are many things to adjust to here and the language is still difficult, I do like it and already feel fairly comfortable. I miss you and think of you every day.

Your younger sister, Sookan

My thoughts were suddenly interrupted by a familiar voice. "Sookan, there you are!" said Ellen. "You missed afternoon attendance. They gave you five demerits for disappearing from the meeting."

I was horrified. I had never gotten a single demerit before! I had been so absorbed with trying to write the letter to my sister that I completely forgot about the meeting.

"Don't worry. It's only demerits," Ellen said. "People get them all the time. I got ten last weekend because Kyle brought me back ten minutes past curfew. It's not that big a deal." She stared down at my letter. "Come on, Sookan. What's the matter? Is everything okay back home?"

I nodded and followed sheepishly, feeling like a criminal for getting demerits. Everyone probably thought I snuck out of the elections on purpose.

Chapter Nine

The next day, Ellen and I took the train to her parents' farmhouse in New Jersey. While Ellen dozed off, I decided to write a letter to Mother.

Dearest Mother,

My roommate, Ellen Lloyd, and I are on our way to her home for Thanksgiving weekend. Thanksgiving is a big holiday here. It's a fall harvest festival, like Chusok in Korea. Everyone goes home to be with family. I'm bringing Ellen's mother some of the lovely hand towels you embroidered. I know she will love them. Handmade goods are especially treasured here.

I am doing well and hope no one is anxious about me. Everything is fine here and I have all that I need. So please don't ever worry about sending me anything.

Did I tell you how much everyone loves to see me dressed in the hanboks you made? I've already worn them several times. The nuns keep asking me to wear them to Sunday Mass. Also, the college administration office often calls me and asks me to wear a hanbok to greet parents and special guests. Many of my classmates and even the nuns come up to me to touch my dress and admire your embroidery. I tell everyone that you made it. My roommate likes the outfits so much that I am thinking of giving one to her. I hope it is all right with you.

The first few times I wore a hanbok on campus, I felt awkward and strange because I stood out so much. But now I am used to it. I know I will always be different and that people will always be curious about me. It is quite a responsibility being the only Korean in my class, for I want to make a good impression so that Americans will think well of Koreans. I want to make everyone at home proud of me.

I hope you are not working too hard, and that you are not still carrying so many things to the convent. I can't help worrying about you.

Your loving daughter, Sookan

When we arrived at the station, Ellen's parents were already waiting for us. I thought Ellen was the luckiest person on earth to have both her parents there waiting to greet her. They rushed over as we stepped off the train, and they each gave me a big hug as Ellen introduced me. I was suddenly lonely for my mother and brothers. I would not see them for four years; it was too far and too expensive for me to visit home.

The Lloyds' large wood-frame farmhouse sat in the middle of an enormous field that seemed endless. As Ellen's mother watched me survey the land, she said, "We have sixteen acres here. The house and all the land used to belong to my grandfather. He built the house and barn himself. You and Ellen will have to go for a long walk this weekend."

Kyle arrived a few hours later, and Ellen's parents seemed delighted to meet their daughter's boyfriend. Kyle was warm and friendly. He enveloped my hand in his big palm and shook it for a while, then said, "Good to meet you, Sookan. Ellen tells me you are a wonderful roommate and a great listener!"

"Maybe because I'm never in our room, and when I am, I fall asleep while she is talking to me," I said.

"Sookan, she puts me to sleep, too," said Ellen's father with a smile.

Ellen laughed and pretended to pout at her father. Her father winked at me and chuckled joyfully. It was so loving and lighthearted. I don't ever remember giving my father such a look. In Korea, children are not even supposed to look grownups in the eye. We love our parents, but the way we express our love and respect is much more restrained and prescribed.

Mrs. Lloyd beamed at Kyle. I could almost hear her thinking, *What a fine young man for Ellen to date while she is in college.* And after Mr. Lloyd fixed Kyle a drink, the two men talked and laughed like old friends. How refreshing it was for me to see them so relaxed at their first meeting. In Korea, it would be inconceivable to bring a boyfriend home for a holiday dinner; only husbands, and maybe fiancés, were allowed.

As Ellen's mother got up to begin serving dinner, Ellen said, "Oh, Mom, wait. Sookan and I have a surprise for all of you. We need to go upstairs for a while. Can you hold dinner just a bit longer?"

Before her mother could answer, Ellen dashed up the creaky stairs, pulling me by the hand. In her room, she quickly put on the *hanbok* I had brought. She had seen me do this many times, and knew exactly how to wear it. I smiled as I watched her struggle with the bow, though, and went to fix it for her so that it would hang properly. We then pulled her hair up in a sweep. With her creamy white skin, blue eyes, and golden hair, she looked splendid in the deep blue *hanbok*. The long skirt hung beautifully on her, and the silver cranes embroidered on the hem seemed to take flight as she twirled around in front of the mirror.

"Ellen, you look stunning! It fits you perfectly," I said. "It's yours. You must keep it."

"I couldn't possibly! Your mother made it for you. And it's too expensive to give away. It's all silk," she said.

"I have three others. If my mother saw you, she would insist you keep it. Besides, you look so beautiful in it that I wouldn't think of wearing it anymore."

"Thank you so much!" she said, giving me a big squeeze and a kiss. "I do look gorgeous, don't I?"

"Yes, you certainly do, Ellen." I beamed at her. It was the first time I had heard any girl declare her own beauty, and I liked it. In Korea, it is considered rude and shallow to compliment oneself. The proper answer would be, "No, I am not beautiful; it is the dress that is beautiful."

To tease Ellen, I repeated the things my mother used to say when I was little and got all dressed up in my *hanbok*. In a stern voice, I said, "Lower your head, young lady, and fold your hands gracefully in front of you. Now take small, delicate steps, and hold your *chima* just so." Ellen looked at me wide-eyed, then played along by following my direction. She bowed deeply to me, and we both burst out laughing.

"Let's go show the others," Ellen said. "Wait, let me compose myself as you said . . . for the full effect, you know." She gingerly made her way down the stairs in her long gown. As I skipped down after her in my comfortable skirt and blouse, I thought about what our college physical education teacher always instructed us to do: "Chest out, shoulders back, chin up." What a difference from the Korean way, which I had just explained to Ellen.

As we appeared, a hush fell over the room. "Look at our little princess," Mrs. Lloyd finally exclaimed with surprise. Kyle could not take his eyes off Ellen, and sensing his gaze, she acted even more demure, playing the enchanted princess from a faraway land.

Suddenly, her father broke into a guffaw. "Ellen, I never knew you could be silent for so long!"

"I can't act like myself while dressed this way, can I?" We all laughed, but I wondered if she had just hit on the reason I was reluctant to wear my *hanbok* on campus.

After dessert, Mrs. Lloyd said, "Oh, Sookan, I have something for you." She hurried to her room and brought out a large maroon book. "Here, open it. Making scrapbooks is sort of a hobby of mine. I kept seeing you in the school newsletter, so I cut the articles out and started a scrapbook for you. I thought you might like to have all these to send home to your family."

As I flipped through the pages, I saw a picture of me in my *hanbok* speaking to the Girl Scouts, another picture of me talking to the local Ladies Garden Club, and a big clipping of me greeting visitors to the school. I had seen the photos in the school newsletters, but I hadn't thought to save them. Now, though, I was glad to be able to look back on what I had done over the past three months. I thanked Mrs. Lloyd for the thoughtful gift. She hadn't even met me until today, and she had been clipping articles since the first day I moved in with Ellen!

As I continued to look through the scrapbook, Mrs. Lloyd said, "Your family must be so proud of you. You have become quite an excellent ambassador for your country, and have made lots of friends, I hear."

It felt so good to hear her say all these nice things. In Korea, elders did not bestow such generous compliments. Young people were *expected* to do well, and it was their

71

job not to disappoint their elders. After spending so much time worrying about disappointing my sister, I appreciated hearing that I had done something right lately.

"Sookan, are you feeling all right?" Mrs. Lloyd asked. "You're looking terribly pale all of a sudden."

"Oh, yes, I'm fine. I think it's just the excitement of my first Thanksgiving."

"No, she's not fine," Ellen piped in. "She's been running herself ragged. I told you she waitresses at the dining hall every weekday evening, then she sneaks out of the room and spends half the night studying. And she spends her weekends baby-sitting or working at the administration office."

Mrs. Lloyd placed her hand on my shoulder and said firmly, "Now, Sookan, I order you to go upstairs and sleep. You need to get some rest this weekend."

I was a bit embarrassed, but I thanked her and hurried to bed, trying to fight back tears. Her concerned, motherly voice was so comforting. I realized how very much I missed my own mother, and how lonesome I had been despite all the new friends I had made. Suddenly I felt the exhaustion of all the sleepless nights and attempts to fit in at school. I pulled the covers over my head, and sobbed until I fell asleep.

Chapter Ten

I heard the alarm clock go off, reached under the bed for the flashlight I kept hidden, and shined the beam on my wristwatch. It was five minutes to four o'clock and I had to get up to study. I hadn't touched any of the books that I had taken to the Lloyds over vacation. Mrs. Lloyd had made sure I rested the whole weekend, and though all the sleep did make me feel a little bit better, I had been back at school for several weeks and now had more work than ever.

Ellen was a heavy sleeper and fortunately never heard my alarm clock, but since she was sensitive to light, I couldn't work at my desk. I grabbed my pillow and blanket, and tiptoed upstairs to my usual spot. At the end of the hall was the shower room, the only room in the building where the lights were kept on all night. There, at the end of the long row of showers, were five sparkling clean bathtubs. I headed to the tub in the corner and spread out my blanket, placed my pillow at the back, and laid my books on the floor. I had discovered this spot the second week of school, and was a regular here. We weren't supposed to leave our rooms after the "lights out" bell, but I felt confident that no one would find me.

I picked up my book for Greek and Roman culture, and began madly flipping through my dictionary. I still had a hundred pages to go, and I had to finish before six, when people would arrive for their morning showers. I just had to make sure not to fall asleep. No one must ever find me here.

I kept pushing ahead with my reading, but I didn't feel right. My head was pounding, and my stomach was all tied up in knots. I pulled my knees into my chest, and kept reading. In order to pull my grade up, I needed a B on today's test. First semester report cards would be sent home soon, and I worried that my grades would shock my family. I had never gotten anything lower than an A− in Korea, but here, I would be lucky if I passed my courses. If only I didn't have to look up so many words; it took so long. The minutes ticked by too quickly and I still had ninety pages to read.

Suddenly, my head started spinning, and I felt a sharp pain in my stomach. I tried to rub the pain away, but it just kept getting worse. Everything seemed blurry. Terrified, I began to gather my books, pillow, and blanket. I had to get back to my room. As I stepped out of the tub, I felt myself fall, and watched the pillow, blanket, and all my books go flying across the floor.

I smelled antiseptic. Slowly, I lifted my heavy eyelids. The curtains were drawn, but the bright December sun cast a soft light on the walls of this quiet room. I looked over and saw an empty bed next to me. I had been in this room before. I had visited Ellen here when she had had the flu. It was so quiet, though. I wondered how long I had been here in the infirmary. I wondered if everyone had already left for Christmas vacation. I tried to sit up, but I felt too dizzy. I gave up and put my head back on the pillow.

"Ah, you're finally awake," Sister Reed said as she entered. "Your fever broke and you had a good rest. You will be fine now." She was carrying a large tray with a bowl of soup, some crackers, a glass of juice, and a vase filled with roses, carnations, and mums.

The scent of cut flowers and chicken soup comforted me. Overwhelmed by the attention, I awkwardly struggled to sit up.

"No, no, no, just lie still," Sister Reed urged. "You are better now, but not well enough to be up and about. Tomorrow, you will be fine. You fainted two days ago and you've been here ever since. Doctor McCormack has been in to check on you several times, and he says you are suffering from exhaustion. He gave you a strong sedative so that you would rest."

"I'm sorry I worried you, Sister Reed," I said as I tried to clear my scratchy throat. What a commotion I must have made so early in the morning.

"Don't fret about that, dear. We were just glad that we found you right away. Ginny Lake was heading in for an early shower, and she heard a big thud. She found you on the floor and called us immediately. I'm so relieved you weren't hurt." She patted my arm. "Doctor McCormack will be back this afternoon to look in on you, but you look much better today. Do you feel up to eating? Here, first try sipping some orange juice through this straw."

As Sister Reed watched me eat, she told me that Christmas vacation had started the day before. She had turned Ellen and Marci away so many times, she said, that they finally listened to her and went home but have been calling often. The flowers had come from the Bennetts, she added.

I started to sob.

"My dear," Sister Reed said as she bent over and kissed me on the forehead, "there is nothing to be concerned about. You are all right and the only thing you have to do now is get plenty of sleep. That will please me immensely. Don't you worry about a thing." She then brushed my hair off my face, pulled the blankets up around me, and quietly left. But I knew that as soon as I felt better, I would be in for a very long talk with her. As both a foreign and scholarship student, I was required to check in with her once a month. Each time, I had told her how much I was enjoying everything, and that I was managing just fine. I had always assured her that things were not too overwhelming or difficult. But our next visit would be different. I knew she would give me a lecture and ask me lots of questions. She would be watching me carefully from now on.

I had ruined everything for myself. I had failed Greek and Roman culture; I hadn't even taken the exam. My family would be crushed and angry when they saw my report card. I had assured them that I wasn't too young to study in America, and that I could handle it. Everything was a mess. I cried myself to sleep.

When I woke up, Marci was quietly sitting and reading beside me. She smiled. "Hey, sleepyhead. You were mumbling something about your report card and Sister Reed. And you were saying a lot of things in Korean. Were you dreaming? You shouldn't be worrying about that stuff now."

"Marci! Have you been here long?" I sat up and found I was feeling much better already.

"Oh, I've been here for about an hour. You look okay. I was really worried. I tried to come and see you a couple of times, but Sister Reed was guarding you and wouldn't even let me in. She asked me a lot of questions about you, too. I was so nervous I can't even remember half of what I said. I had to answer her, though. I hope you don't mind."

I couldn't help smiling. Marci wasn't fond of any of the nuns here and I could imagine how nervous she must have been when Sister Reed, with her piercing green eyes, interrogated her.

"Oh, that's all right, Marci. I am a bit afraid of her, but I know she cares for me a lot. I'm already starting to brace myself for the lecture I'm going to get from her. I assumed she had already heard about my sneaking up to the bathroom to study every night. And I bet Ellen told her that I haven't been to one mixer."

"Oh, Ellen was so upset. She told Sister Reed she wanted to sleep in the bed next to you and wait for you to wake up. Sister Reed sent her home and told her to call. She sent me home, too, but that's no big deal since I can just drive right over."

After one more day in the infirmary, Doctor McCormack told Sister Reed that I could leave as long as I took it easy.

"Marci will be here to take you to her house for Christmas vacation just as you both had planned," said Sister Reed, to my great surprise. "Ellen has called for you several times, but I thought it best that you rest. You can give her a call a little later. Maybe you and Marci and Ellen can all get together over vacation. Now, there is one condition. You are not to take any books with you to Marci's. In January, when you return, we will discuss your schedule."

Marci came running in. "This is great; you can come home with me now. I went by and got your mail for you. I'm just going to swing by the library and return some books, and then I'll come back and get you, okay?"

Chapter Eleven

There were letters from my mother and sister, and two pieces of folded construction paper that I knew were from little Sarah and Jimmy. I unfolded the piece of red construction paper; it was Sarah's. She had drawn a jolly Santa Claus saying, "Hi, Sookan, what do you want for Christmas? I don't know what you want. Can you tell me? From your Santa."

Jimmy had used green paper, and in black crayon, he had written: "St. Nick is coming. Our tree is all decorated. Will you come to see it?" Underneath, he had drawn a huge tree, groaning under the weight of all the decorations hanging from its limbs.

I realized that Christmas was only a few days away, and I didn't have gifts for anyone. I did still have a few things that I had brought from home. Mother had embroidered several hand towels for me to give as gifts. I knew Mrs. Bennett would like those. I had also brought a hand-carved wooden tiger, which Jimmy might enjoy. For Sarah, though, I had nothing. In a shop in town I had noticed a small china figurine of a little girl holding flowers. Sarah might like that. But I didn't have much money saved up, and what would I give to Marci and Ellen? I thought of the soft leather handbag I had wanted to buy for Mother, and the anatomy book I had intended to give Inchun. Perhaps over Christmas vacation I could earn enough money to buy these things and could mail them off in January. But how? I would be with Marci the whole time.

I opened Mother's letter.

My dear Sookan,

I am comforted to know that you are adjusting well to your new home and have already made some good friends. Young people learn everything so quickly. Since I am so far away from you and cannot understand all that you are facing, I feel that I can provide you with little advice. Hyunchun told me there is an English expression about doing things like a Roman when you are in Rome. I thought that expression was very wise. My main concern is that you always want to do everything so perfectly all the time. Give yourself some time. Struggling to do everything perfectly according to Korean and American tradition all at the same time will be too much for you. Now, you are a student in America, and you should enjoy your life there. Do not worry about things at home. I know how you fret about your brothers and me. You are such a worrywart. You always were. But all is well here.

Mrs. Na, the go-between, was over at the house earlier today. She brought several more pictures of potential brides for Hanchun. She insisted that I pick one, but I told her that Hanchun is not interested in marriage yet, nor are my second and third sons, and she must wait a little longer. She said she would be back in a few weeks. She is not likely to give up on me as I have three sons of marriageable age. I know you don't like her much, but she has made some very good matches. Of course, your aunts and uncles are also busy recommending girls from good families. So far, I am not pursuing any of this, and all is pretty much the same.

Hyunchun is now busier than ever. He was elected student body president and he also took on an extra job at the American Embassy as a clerk. He comes home at midnight most of the week.

Oh, a bit of news about Bokhi. She used to come by and chat with me, hoping to get a glimpse of Hyunchun. I always enjoyed her visits. She used to read all your letters and we would speak of you. She told me that she thinks of you every day, but finds it hard to write. She misses you too much and she said words are hardly adequate to express her feelings. But I am sure she will write one of these days.

We have not seen much of her lately. She has a lot of responsibilities at home. Her old aunt and many nephews keep her frightfully busy. Also, her family did not think it was proper for Bokhi to come to our house so often, and I can certainly understand that. Bokhi's aunt is looking for a suitable husband for her. I know she is in love with Hyunchun, but it would not work. Hyunchun has two elder brothers who need to be married first. His turn will not come for quite some time. My heart aches for Bokhi and I know Hyunchun feels bad about it, too. But time is not on their side. There is nothing for you to do and please do not worry. These things take their own course, and all will work out in the end. Marriages are complex family matters. I will do all I can to comfort Bokhi as you would. I thought you would like to know.

Promise me that you will look after yourself. Your brothers send their best. I saw Hyunchun writing you a letter, but I doubt he will ever finish it and mail it. That is just the way he is. None of them is a good correspondent, I'm afraid. I know Inchun thinks of you often, though he hardly ever says a thing. When we read your letters aloud, he acts like he is not even paying attention, but later, he wanders around whistling, picks the letter up, and goes to his room. Whenever I visit Theresa, I first have to go into his drawer and get your letters out. But I always put them back when I return.

By the time you receive this letter, it will be Christmastime. Your brothers and I are going to attend midnight Mass at Myungdong Cathedral. Will you be spending the vacation with your roommate's family? Have a merry Christmas.

Your loving mother

Tears filled my eyes. I missed Mother, and wished I could hug her, or sit with her in the kitchen and just talk to her. She always worked so hard, and never uttered a word of complaint. I think I was the only one who understood her. My brothers were always out, and my sister only saw Mother for brief visits. Now Bokhi wouldn't be there either.

Why couldn't Bokhi continue to come by and get to know Hyunchun? They could wait for each other. Traditions and customs! I could tell Mother felt for the two of them, yet there was nothing she could do.

I knew Mother. I saw how sad and pensive she looked when she thought no one was around. I used to hear her sigh as she worked late into the night while the rest of us were in bed. Sometimes, I would go to her room late at night, and I would see her sitting up straight, staring at the moon as if she were searching for someone. I knew she needed someone to talk to, but when I went to her at those times, she would just hug me and tell me to go back to bed. I knew she thought I was too young to understand.

Without Father, she needed her eldest daughter to talk to, but Theresa was busy with her work at the convent. Mother would stay up half the night cooking or sewing things for the nuns before we made our monthly visits to the convent. She always worked too hard. The last time I went with her, she had stayed up the entire night making layers and layers of rice cakes to feed the nuns, all one hundred of them. We carried the heavy containers of rice cakes onto the crowded bus and then all the way up the hill to the convent. As I watched Mother perspiring and stopping to catch her breath, I got so angry that I shouted, "Why couldn't we bring a small package just for Theresa?" But Mother had answered, "It is a convent and they are all my daughters."

I didn't say another word about it, especially not to my brothers. They would have scolded me and told me that I was rude and disrespectful. We had to support our older sister and the nuns who worked so hard, I knew they would have said. I often wondered if I were not as kind-hearted as the rest of my family.

Although I loved my sister and admired her hard work for the poor, I didn't like the way she upset Mother all the time by telling her of her hardships at the convent. Mother had so little herself that I resented my sister's unending demands. I did not understand my sister sometimes. I promised myself that I would not be like her, that I would take care of my problems on my own. Mother did not need anyone giving her more worries. I began to read my sister's letter.

To my dear younger sister,

My work never ends. Each day I toil from dawn to dusk, and still there is so much more to do. So many poor people need our help.

I received your letter. You seem very much taken with the independence and outspokenness of American young people. And you were unduly impressed by your professor's cooking for his family. Please remember that you are at an impressionable age. You must think long and carefully about these new attitudes and ideas before you embrace them with such enthusiasm. You also seem to be quite chatty. You must be in the habit of talking a great deal with your college friends. Remember that a young woman must spare her words and think carefully before she speaks.

I feel that you may have left home too early. You must not forget the beauty of our traditions and culture. Our ways are not always easy, but the values which we maintain are so important. Remember that family is one of the most important things in your life. Doing your duties as a younger sister is sometimes difficult, but your older brothers have done many things for you, and you must honor and respect them. And you must be a worthy big sister to Inchun. When you return to Korea and join me, your brothers will be proud, knowing that you are helping to do God's work.

Christmas is coming soon. There are so many supplies which we need here for the students. I have made a list of some of the important items we need so that you can send them. As for our family, you should send Mother and each of our brothers a thoughtful gift from America.

Remember, my dear Sookan, that you must not be swept away by the new culture you are in. You are Korean, and your home is here. If you embrace your new culture too fervently, you will later feel lost. You will be neither American nor Korean anymore. I do not want to see this happen to you. I am disappointed. I thought you were stronger and more mature.

I hope you will take some time to think about things. Pray to God for His help.

I remain your loving sister.

I stared at her letter and the list of supplies. She had told me to share my feelings and experiences, and now she did not approve of the way I saw my new world. She did not like what I was becoming. I had made a point of writing her a cheerful letter — even got five demerits for writing it — and she thought I seemed too talkative and silly.

I sighed, folded the letter, and put it back in the envelope. She didn't understand me. She didn't respect me. And why did she have to remind me to get Christmas presents for my brothers? Doesn't she know that I love them all? Does she think that I love them less now that I am far away? Does she think that I left home because I didn't care for them? I wondered if she really loved *me* the way she always said she did.

But as soon as I thought these things, I felt guilty. It was probably my fault. I had not been completely honest with her about my life here. She obviously thought that everything was being provided to me by the school, and that I spent all my time chatting with my friends. But what was the sense of worrying everyone at home? They couldn't help.

I reread the letter. *Is she right? Have I changed so much in the past three months? Will I be sorry later, when I no longer fit in at home?* All I knew was that I was trying as best I could to make everyone proud of me.

Chapter Twelve

Our footsteps echoed as Marci and I walked down the hall of the empty dorm. I felt a bit dizzy and tired still, but was happy finally to be spending some time with Marci.

"Do you mind if we just stay here one more night?" I asked her. "I feel like I've been away for a long time, and I'm sure I have to return some books and clean my room a bit. I also need to go downtown to get something."

"No problem," Marci said. "My parents won't be back from Europe till the day after tomorrow. I can go with you. What do you have to get?"

"Oh, something small for Sarah. Then maybe we can drop it off at the Bennetts' before we go to your house. I just want to see them before I leave. With all these papers and exams, I wasn't able to baby-sit last weekend. I feel like I haven't seen them for a long time."

Marci drove me downtown to buy the porcelain figurine for Sarah. I had already wrapped Mrs. Bennett's present and Jimmy's, but I still didn't have anything for Professor Bennett, or for Marci and Ellen, and I had little money left. I wanted to do something for all of them, but just didn't know how I possibly could.

I thought of Mother, who I knew would be preparing a big Christmas dinner. How she loved to watch the family and her guests enjoy the meal she had prepared. Everyone looked forward to our Christmas feasts. Mother was a wonderful cook, and the conversation always went on for hours. I wondered if I could make people happy as she did. I wondered if I could cook, for I had never really tried before. I had always just watched Mother, and helped serve and clean up.

Maybe I could do it. I could make a big dinner and invite the Bennetts, Marci, and Ellen to a party at the dorm. There was a small kitchen on the first floor, and in the parlor, a decorated Christmas tree. The dorm was empty, so Jimmy and Sarah could run around all they wanted. The more I thought about it, the better it sounded. I wondered if they would like Korean food. Would it be too strange for them? And would I be able to make it? I wasn't sure, but I was determined to do something special for everyone.

"Marci, do you know where can I buy groceries? I need rice, beef, carrots, eggs, cucumbers . . . Let's see . . . scallions, honey, pears . . . oh, and soy sauce and sesame oil."

"What for?" Marci asked, rather surprised.

"Well, I want to make a delicious Korean dinner for you, Ellen, and the Bennetts. I thought we could have a Christmas party in the dorm." I hoped that I could deliver on the "delicious" aspect. I'd be lucky if it were edible.

"You just got out of the infirmary. You're not strong enough to cook."

"Oh, I feel okay. I'm just a bit tired. And I'm suddenly homesick for Korean food. It will make me happy to see everyone eating what I make. Besides, you'll be there to help me."

"I don't know how to cook. You do?" Marci asked.

"Well, I think so," I said. "First, we'll have to find all the ingredients."

"You sure we can have the party in the dorm?"

"Oh, yes. Sister Casey won't mind. Last weekend, I saw Jean baking cookies in the kitchen. But we'll double-check with her anyway."

We called everyone and scheduled the dinner for the following day. I had been worried that Ellen might not be able to make it since it was a bit of a drive, but she said that she and Kyle wouldn't miss it. Marci and I found most of the ingredients at the grocery store, but we had to drive all over town before we found a small Far Eastern food store that had sesame oil and soy sauce. That night, Marci slept in Ellen's bed to watch over me and make sure I slept.

Trying hard to remember all the things I had watched Mother do, I sliced the beef into very thin, bite-sized pieces, and marinated them in soy sauce, honey, sesame oil, ground pear, garlic, black pepper, and chopped scallions. Meanwhile, I julienned cucumbers and more pears to make Mother's special salad. Not quite sure of how much seasoning to use, I kept tasting it to make sure it was all right. Marci, who stood and watched at first, started tasting things, too, and offering her suggestions about the right blend of ingredients. When everything was almost ready, she began baking brownies. At the grocery store, I had told Marci that Koreans usually have fruit for dessert, but she didn't think that would do at all for a Christmas dinner, so she had bought a brownie mix. With the beef cooking, and Marci's brownies baking, the dorm room smelled wonderfully inviting. I fed her a piece of meat and a big spoonful of hot rice to taste.

"Mmm, this is great!" she mumbled through her food.

"Oh, I am so glad," I said with satisfaction.

Ellen and Kyle came in with three shopping bags, a poinsettia, and some cut flowers. Marci smiled shyly as she shook Kyle's hand.

"Now, I'm here, so you go sit down," Ellen said to me. "You should not be doing all this. Sister Reed wouldn't even let me talk to you the other day. Let me take a look at you."

"I'm fine now. Sorry to have worried you. And thanks for coming."

"It smells terrific! What's it called?" she said.

"*Bulgogi*," I answered, staring proudly at the platter of marinated, grilled beef I had prepared.

"I can't wait to taste it," Ellen said enthusiastically.

"Let me get this table set." Then she pulled a red tablecloth and matching napkins from one of her bags. Out of another bag came Christmas serving plates, onto which she started transferring the rice, *bulgogi*, and vegetables.

It was just like Ellen to color coordinate the whole dinner table. The simple food I made now looked so festive and grand. I smiled proudly, but Marci made a face as if to say that it didn't make that much of a difference. To Marci, all this extra fuss was not necessary as long as the food tasted good. I felt so happy with both of my best friends there.

I placed the few little presents I had for the Bennetts under the tree. Ellen ran up to our room and brought down her little phonograph to play Christmas music. Suddenly, the huge, empty dorm felt warm and welcoming. Marci, Ellen, and I had no gifts to exchange, but in a strange way, it was even more special that way. It made our silent gift of friendship even more meaningful. No present could have given us more joy than looking around at our afternoon's accomplishment.

I heard Jimmy and Sarah charging into the dorm.

"Hey, it's empty! Look how big this place is," Sarah squealed.

"Something smells wonderful. Let's follow our noses," I heard Mrs. Bennett say. We met them at the entrance to the parlor, and Sarah gave me a big kiss.

"Look, Jimmy. Look at the Korean food Sookan has made," Professor Bennett said.

"And Marci, too," I added. "She helped me with the Korean dishes and then made the brownies. And Ellen brought the Christmas butter cookies and she set this beautiful table."

As I introduced Marci, Ellen, and Kyle to the Bennetts, Sister Casey came by to see how we were doing. "Oh, what a wonderful party!" she said. Of course, we told her she must join us.

To my great relief, everyone seemed to like the *bulgogi*, the salad, and the sticky white rice. When Mrs. Bennett asked for the recipes, I didn't know what to say. "I will have to come over and make it for you. Marci and I used our taste buds instead of a recipe," I finally confessed.

Sister Reed walked into the dorm, looking for Sister Casey, and saw me. "Sookan, are you still here? What in the world is going on with this child? You were told to leave campus and rest," she said.

"I'm sorry, Sister Reed," said Sister Casey. "These two insisted on using the kitchen."

"What a stubborn girl," she said, shaking her head at me. "Full of surprises. Well, what is that delicious smell?" We quickly set a place for her, and she smiled warmly as she sat down to eat.

It was glorious to see everyone enjoying the food. I finally understood why Mother loved having people over for dinner. As we ate, Mrs. Bennett told Sister Reed how wonderful I was with the children, and how the whole family loved me. Marci and Ellen winked at me from across the table as I blushed and smiled awkwardly. *What a marvelous thing a wink is; without a sound, one can convey so much,* I thought.

Sister Reed got out of her chair and walked toward me with her arms outstretched. "Merry Christmas, my dear!" she whispered as she gave me a big hug. "You are a naughty child, but I must admit you have done well. Perhaps this was what you needed: some of your favorite foods and your friends with you. I'm very proud of you."

"Merry Christmas, Sister Reed, and thank you for your care and support." My voice trembled. Her words of encouragement were magical to me. I would always remember her, and I hoped that someday, I would be able to make a young girl feel as proud and happy as she had made me.

Chapter Thirteen

It was Christmas Eve, and Marci's parents had just returned from their trip to Europe. Mr. Gannon, a tall, handsome man with cool gray eyes, was impeccably dressed in a pinstripe suit and wingtip shoes. Mrs. Gannon was a regal woman with sparkling blue eyes. Her hair was curled under, with not a single strand out of place. She looked as if she had just come from the beauty parlor. As Marci introduced me, her parents shook my hand and ushered me into their spacious living room, where a collection of modern art and sculpture was elegantly displayed.

"You are a little later than we expected," Mrs. Gannon said. "Martha has dinner all ready, so we should probably sit down right away." We settled ourselves in the dimly lit dining room, and the butler began to bustle around. As we sat in silence, I looked over at Marci. Her head was lowered and she was quickly eating her soup. I felt uncomfortable and wondered if it was a good idea for me to have come home with her.

"Marci, college has certainly not improved your manners," her mother said. "Sit up straight, and please don't gobble your food. Dad and I would love to hear about school. How did the end of the term go?"

"Everything is fine. Nothing's new. Same old stuff," Marci responded, not even bothering to look up.

Mrs. Gannon blanched and Mr. Gannon, like Marci, silently ate his soup.

Forcing a smile, Mrs. Gannon said, "Marci, dear, Dad and I were thinking the three of us should go on a cruise this summer. Wouldn't that be nice? You could get a little color!"

"No, Mother. I have other things I want to do this summer," Marci answered flatly.

I realized she didn't discuss anything with her parents. She had recently dropped out of one of her classics courses, deciding to take it the next year. And she was planning on going to Greece for the summer. Her parents did not seem to know any of this. Mr. Gannon's jaw was clenched as he stared coolly at his daughter.

Marci began to butter a roll in silence, but I saw a deep furrow in her brow.

"So, Sookan," Mr. Gannon said to me, "you have come from Korea, I understand. What kind of food do you eat there on a day like today?"

I had been asked this kind of question so many times that I was readily able to give him a detailed list of the sorts of dishes Mother prepared on special occasions. I next answered his questions about the weather, explaining that we had four seasons just like New York, but that in the summer there was a monsoon period that was very rainy and humid. We covered the full litany of questions that I was used to getting about Korea's land, its people, the customs, and traditions.

I answered all his questions at great length, wanting to fill the silence for as long as possible. But it was awkward. I knew he was not really interested, and that no one was paying attention to what I was saying. If anything, I think Mr. Gannon was wondering why Marci had befriended me and brought me home. He seemed to look at me with both curiosity and disdain. I tried not to look in his direction as I continued speaking. I kept glancing over at Marci, who remained bent over her plate, eating with determination.

Then, the maid brought out a huge silver platter of duck in orange sauce.

"Have you ever had such a fine-looking duck, Sookan?" Mr. Gannon asked. "Perhaps you don't have these kinds of things in Korea. I understand it is a very poor country, with the war and all. That must have been difficult for you."

I was getting more and more uncomfortable. I didn't want to think about the war; I didn't want to talk about losing my father and so many of my friends just to entertain everyone. I wished he would talk to me about art, or Europe, or college life. It was as if he thought I didn't know about anything except the "poor" country I was from.

"Actually, I've never eaten duck before. Mother and I raise ducks as pets. We have a beautiful pond in our

97

backyard where the ducks swim. We would never eat them," I said. "For special occasions or for dinner parties, Mother often serves quail or pheasant. She's a wonderful cook, and loves to entertain. Everyone stays late into the night eating, talking, and laughing."

I didn't like Mr. Gannon's condescending attitude toward me, but I immediately felt awful for trying to show off and insult him. I should have politely said that I loved duck and that it looked delicious. I knew my sister would have scolded me if she had seen me behave this way. I looked sheepishly at Marci and thought I saw her grin.

Mrs. Gannon continued eating her salad, seemingly undisturbed. She cheerfully said, "Marci, honey, I can take you and Sookan to the beauty parlor and have Louis cut your hair. You need a new haircut; you look like a boy. And we'll have Sandra develop a new makeup regimen for you."

"Mom, I still have a large box of makeup that Sandra sold us last time I was home. I don't care for that stuff. I'm not like Susan," Marci snapped.

"Marci" — Mrs. Gannon faltered — "I just want you to look pretty for your formal dinners at the dining hall. I ran into Mrs. Montgomery and Anne a couple of weekends ago, and Anne was telling me how elegant the dinners at Finch College are, and how she loves getting all dressed up. It sounds wonderful. You never mentioned that to me. I know of some fabulous little boutiques that we can go to for cocktail dresses."

"Well, I didn't mention it because I think it's a tremendous bother and a waste of time. I don't care for that type of thing. I prefer the snack bar."

" 'I don't care for this . . . I don't care for that . . .' Is that all you can say?" Her father roared. "Do you realize I pay for that fancy college dinner only to have you go and spend money on greasy snack bar food? Why do I bother sending you to an expensive college?"

Marci ignored him and kept eating.

There was a long silence, and it was clear that Mr. Gannon was trying to regain his composure. He finally said, "Marci, did you give a minute's thought to what we talked about last time? About your majoring in chemistry and working with me this summer? You might even like it. Why not at least try?"

"Dad, for the hundredth time, I do not like chemistry. I'm not good at it. Please don't ever tell me again that I have to take over Gannon Chemical someday."

"Not good at it! How do you know if you don't try? All you seem to do now is read Greek tragedies. No wonder you look so pale and somber." His hands were shaking, and his right eye twitched. "I want to see my daughter thriving and enjoying life! What happened to that fancy camera I bought you? Have you even tried it? I wanted to display your photography at my office. I wanted to show you off."

"I haven't taken any good pictures yet. I haven't gotten around to it."

Mr. Gannon banged on the table and shouted, "Damn it, Marci! Look at me when you speak to me."

I was stunned. I didn't know what to do. Mrs. Gannon sighed, and said, "Marci, dear, you apologize to your father."

Marci stood up and threw her spoon across the table. "You always take his side. You've been traveling the world, leaving me home alone with Martha ever since I can remember. Do you have to humiliate me when I bring my best friend home for Christmas? I should have known it would be a mistake. Come on, Sookan, let's go upstairs to my room."

I had never seen a young person speak to her parents that way. I was so startled by the whole exchange that I couldn't move. I just sat there and stared at Mr. Gannon. He watched Marci storm up the stairs, and his expression grew dark. I saw his cool, cavalier façade crumble. He seemed dejected and helpless. He looked into my eyes, searching for something that would help him understand.

"I'll bet you'd never talk back to your father like that," he said in a low voice. "In Asia, you listen to your parents, don't you? Children in this country can learn a few things from you."

"Dear, don't worry," Mrs. Gannon said to him. "She's just going through a rebellious phase. She has always been stubborn like that, ever since she was young. She never seemed to do what we told her to."

I asked them if I could be excused, and ran upstairs to see Marci.

Marci had the entire second floor to herself. In contrast to the downstairs, where every corner housed the appropriate painting or statue, the second floor was practically bare. Marci's room had two beds, a dresser, a mirror, bookshelves, and a large poster of the Greek Pantheon.

Marci was staring out the window, puffing on a cigarette. "Want one?" she said, turning toward me.

"No, thanks."

"Why not? Try it!" Marci dared me. "Just to find out what it's like."

"Does it make you feel better?" I asked.

"Yup. They would hate it if they saw me smoking." She blew a smoke ring into the air. "I'm sorry for ruining your first Christmas dinner in America, Sookan."

"Oh, don't worry about that," I said.

"I guess I should have warned you. We've been having these scenes ever since I was in high school. My parents just want me to be something I'm not. They don't understand that I have my own tastes and interests. I'm just very different from my older sister and from them. I feel like I'm going to burst whenever I'm near them. I think they hate me."

Marci had begun to cry, and quickly wiped her eyes. I couldn't think of anything to say to make her feel better. We sat there in silence, staring out the window.

After a while, I said, "Maybe I *will* try a cigarette. May I have one?" She tossed me the pack, then lit the end of my cigarette with her silver lighter.

"Come on, you have to inhale to get it to light," she said impatiently.

My lips hugged the small cigarette tight and I took a deep breath. I imagined myself tilting my head back and blowing smoke rings at the ceiling like Lauren Bacall. Instead, I started to cough, and I could feel my face turning red. My throat burned and my chest ached. Marci pounded on my back and I stubbed out the cigarette in the ashtray.

She began to laugh. "You make a pathetic smoker," she said. "You know, Sookan, I'm so glad you're here. I really am."

"I know, Marci. I'm glad I'm here, too."

The moon had risen, and we watched the shadows of the falling snow. I pulled a blanket onto the floor, and lay down on my back so I could stare up at the sky. Marci did the same, and we silently watched the snow fall. I felt as though I had known Marci a very long time.

After a long silence, I said, "You know, Marci, I have to tell you something."

"What?" she asked.

"I think you're wrong to believe your father hates you."

"He does. I know he does," she said.

"Marci, he does not. I saw it in his eyes when you stormed out. All of a sudden, he looked so sad. I think he is just impatient for you to enjoy all that he can provide for you."

Marci didn't answer. Maybe I shouldn't have said anything, but I thought she should know what I felt.

After a long while, she said, "Why does he always have to tell me what to do with my life? I'm eighteen now — almost nineteen, actually. I need to live my life. It's *my* life!"

I stared at her thinking how refreshing those words sounded to me. *It's my life.* I had never said those words aloud. I felt it sometimes, but I would never dare speak it.

While I was still savoring her words, Marci said, "Oh, Sookan, you wouldn't understand how frustrating it is to have to deal with someone as domineering and pushy as my father. He wants to control my entire life. He makes me feel guilty for not being like my sister and for not liking chemistry and photography as much as he does."

"But I *do* understand," I said firmly.

"How can you? Your family is a million miles away. You never even see them."

"I wish it were all that simple," I said. "Family pressure has a way of finding you, no matter how far away you are."

Marci looked at me questioningly.

In a rush, I started explaining. "It's my older sister. She has plans for me. She is waiting for me to return to Korea and join the convent, to work side by side with her. Ever since I was little, she has been telling me this. And I always looked up to her, and I always believed that she knew what was best for me. Now, I'm not sure of what I want to do with my life. But, she has her idea of exactly what type of person I should be, and how I should act. And now, I'm disappointing her. I finally wrote and told her about my life here, the things I do, and the things I've seen. She wrote back and said she is worried that I am becoming too American and forgetting Korean traditions and customs. She told me that I am too impressionable and that she is disappointed with me. It's all so confusing for me sometimes. I am just trying to get through the school year. And yet, every day I worry about disappointing everyone back home. I hear you and Ellen saying that you're eighteen years old and have to lead your own lives, but in Korea, it wouldn't matter if I were *fifty* years old. I would still have to obey and respect my elders. It is my duty and obligation. If I fail, I bring shame on myself and on my family. I don't want to disappoint Theresa or the rest of my family, but more and more, I'm not sure that I want to be the type of person my sister wants me to be. I'm not sure anymore that she always knows what is best for me." Out of breath, I fell silent.

"Throw her letters out and don't think about them," Marci said.

"I can't throw them out. I am so far away from home, and I miss my family so much. I miss Theresa, too. I have always been an obedient younger sister. I feel terrible knowing that I am disappointing her and not living up to my duties, but at the same time, I can't help feeling angry toward her for making me feel bad. Then, I keep thinking that it's my own fault. She probably thinks I'm having an easy life in a rich country and that the nuns at school are giving me everything I need."

"Well, why don't you tell her the truth, then?" Marci asked.

"I can't. My mother would worry about me too much. And my brothers would feel even guiltier for not being able to send me any money. Sometimes I wonder if my sister is being hard on me because she knows I am doubting and questioning all sorts of things. In her letter, she told me to think and pray. She also included a list of things I am to send her for her students. I think she wants to keep me busy doing things that will make me remember her and the convent."

"Sookan, your sister sounds very arrogant and controlling," Marci said emphatically. "She thinks she knows everything. But she doesn't know what goes on here, and she can't determine what's best for you. You need to live your own life, not just imitate hers. You have to break free of her."

"But, I can't. I would be a disgrace to my family," I said.

Marci and I sat quietly for a long time, both looking outside and listening to the distant noises from the street.

Chapter Fourteen

Back at school, I spoke to my Greek and Roman culture professor, and, to my great relief, he said he would let me take a makeup exam. Then, I signed up for a visit with Sister Reed.

When I entered her office, she walked me over to her sofa and said, "Sookan, let's sit here and visit for a while. I'm glad to see you looking so much healthier."

As I took my seat, I drew in a deep breath to brace myself for the discussion ahead of me.

"I just got off the phone with Professor Bennett," Sister Reed said. "What do you think of dropping the second half of world literature, and taking it this summer? Professor Bennett will be conducting a summer session. That way, you can do all the assigned reading and actually enjoy those wonderful novels. I hear you already spoke to Miss Mullen about a summer job, and she says she can arrange your hours so that you will be free to attend the world literature lectures."

I thought about it and said, "Thank you for arranging all that. But I'm afraid that I may not have enough credits to meet my freshman requirements and my scholarship might not be renewed. My family would be so disappointed."

"My dear, you needn't worry about that. We all think you are an extraordinary young woman, and we all admire what you have been able to accomplish. Your scholarship is not in jeopardy, I can assure you that. You should not worry about your family either. The college will send a special letter to them along with your first semester's report card. This college does not measure a student's accomplishments by grades alone." She smiled. "If you do want to get more credits this semester, however, I think you might consider taking an art or music course. It would be fun for you — and having fun is important, too. You still have three and a half years ahead of you to take all the courses you want. And as your English continues to improve, the course work will become easier and easier. For this semester, why don't you at least take one class that you can really enjoy?"

I felt numb and could not find anything to say. She had gone to a great deal of trouble, and I was grateful to her for discerning my needs so well. I had been wanting to take a painting class. Every time I walked by the large, sunny art studio and saw the students peacefully working at their canvases, I thought about how lucky they were. I would never have chosen to take painting on my own, for fear that my sister might say I was wasting my time. I was sure she would tell me that I could have taken painting at home, and was missing the opportunity to study more important matters in America.

"Sookan, I hope that this sounds all right to you. I think it will work out well, but you can give it some thought. Now, I have something for you."

Sister Reed went to the tall, wooden file cabinet, unlocked the bottom drawer, then pulled out a red velvet box.

"These are for you," she said. "My aunt gave them to me shortly before she died five years ago. She asked me to make a special present of them on her behalf when I came upon a truly extraordinary young woman. I know she will be happy that I have found someone so deserving. Here, these are your little treasures now."

She had once before told me that I was extraordinary, but I hadn't given it much thought. Now, I was overwhelmed. My hands trembled as I reached out to accept the precious velvet box. I opened it, and could not believe my eyes. A string of cream-colored pearls with a platinum-and-diamond clasp lay gracefully draped in the box. Next to the necklace was a shiny platinum pin in the shape of a wishbone, with a single pearl in its grasp.

"Sister Reed, thank you, but these are too precious for me to take," I said.

"They are perfect for you. I am looking forward to seeing you wear them." She picked up the pin and held it against my chest for a minute. "It looks beautiful on you. Now, put the box in your book bag and I'll let you get back to your busy schedule." She hugged me and gave me a gentle kiss on the forehead.

I didn't tell anyone about Sister Reed's special gift. I went straight over to see Miss Mullen, and signed up for an extra office job on Saturday. I wanted to save up some money to buy a pair of new high heels, and then I would get all dressed up, show Sister Reed, and surprise Ellen at a Friday mixer.

I had half an hour before work at the dining hall, and I decided to write home.

Dear Mother, Older Sister, and Brothers,

I hope you are all well and had a good Christmas and a happy New Year. Forgive me for not writing for so long. I am fine, but have just been very busy here with college life.

Second semester is about to begin. My English has improved some, but I still depend heavily on the dictionaries I brought with me. They are now quite tattered, and I have to handle them carefully. This semester, I will be taking medieval philosophy; Europe in transition, 1453–1815; religions of the world; and painting. I am excited about taking an art class. If my paintings come out well, I plan to give them to my friends Ellen and Marci in June when they both leave for summer vacation.

Let me tell you how I spent Christmas here in

America. For the first time in my life, I cooked a Korean dinner. I wanted to do something special for my roommate, Marci, my English professor and his family, Sister Casey, and Sister Reed. It was a wonderful evening. Everyone seemed to enjoy the food I prepared. I was surprised it turned out so well. Perhaps it tasted all right to me because I have forgotten how delicious Mother's cooking is.

I will write again soon. Meanwhile, I hope everyone is in good health.

> My love to all,
> Sookan

At the dining hall while setting the tables, I heard familiar footsteps charging down the hall, and saw Sarah and Jimmy running toward me.

"Sookan, we looked for you in the library. We went all around the reference room, and through the stacks," chattered Sarah. "We found your book bag, but not you. Mommy said to give this to you." She handed me an envelope.

"No, Sarah is lying," Jimmy said. "Mommy said to leave it with the librarian, but we knew we could find you."

The letter read: "Dear Sookan, We hope that you had a good Christmas vacation, and that you got some much-needed rest. The children miss you. I know you are busy these days, but how about lunch this Saturday? Let me know. Love, Jane."

"Can you, can you?" asked Sarah.

"No, I'm sorry. I already promised I would work at the office all day Saturday." I saw Jimmy peering through the kitchen door, watching Peggy walk in and out of the big freezers. "I can give you a tour of the big kitchen here if you want to see it." I was sure Peggy wouldn't mind if I took a few minutes to show them around since I had arrived early that day.

"Oh, boy, can we walk inside the giant refrigerator?" Jimmy asked.

I held their hands and asked Peggy if I could give them a quick tour. We all promised to be very careful, and she gave us a nod.

As we walked through the kitchen, the chefs, in their tall white hats and long aprons, waved to us and smiled as they diced, chopped, and sautéed. The giant pots were boiling away, and the huge frying pans were sizzling. We opened the door to the freezer room, and Sarah's teeth started chattering.

"We could turn Sarah into a Popsicle," Jimmy exclaimed.

Then we entered the walk-in refrigerator. "Wow, look at all those little balls of butter, and those little cups of grape and strawberry jam. It looks pretty. Who did that?" asked Sarah.

"Me," I said. "I did those yesterday." Sarah looked

very proud to know her friend had done such a thing.

I realized that I missed Jimmy and Sarah. I hadn't been able to baby-sit for them the last couple of weeks, but in a way, I was glad because I was uncomfortable getting paid for having such a good time with them.

"You know what? Next time, I can take you on a tour of the administration building, and I can show you the big rumbling mimeograph machine in the basement."

"Daddy works here, but he never shows us anything. We'll come back tomorrow," Jimmy said as they ran back to report everything to their mother.

Right before dinner, Ellen rushed in and pulled me aside. "Sookan, I just got back from seeing Kyle," she whispered. "Take a look at my hand, but don't utter a word. You're the first one to see it. I'm going to go tell Peggy now, so that she'll announce it. Oh, I am so excited! I always wanted to be the first one in our class to be engaged!"

I just stood and gazed at the large diamond that sparkled on her left hand. I was speechless. Though she always talked about marrying Kyle, it was different to actually see the ring. "What do your parents think?" I asked, unable to come up with anything else.

"My parents are so upset. I called and told them, and they said I should give the ring back. They said I would be ruining my life by jumping into this so soon. But I know Kyle is the one for me. I love him, and I want to marry him."

I stared at Ellen as I tried to absorb what she was

saying. In Korea, by the time a girl wears an engagement ring, several official family meetings have taken place. "Ellen, should you really go ahead and announce this when your parents are so upset with you?"

"It's what I want. I don't know why they can't understand that. They liked Kyle when they met him over Thanksgiving. I am so mad at both of them that I told Kyle I feel like eloping right away. Sookan, don't look so glum, and let's not talk about my parents anymore. Be happy for me. When I get married, I want you to be my maid of honor."

I managed a small smile and said, "Ellen, I *am* happy for you, but I can't help worrying about your parents. There is no need to hurt them. And I know you won't be happy if they're not happy, too."

Her smile dissolved and she suddenly looked as if she would burst into tears.

"Ellen, I'm sure it will all work out all right," I said, sorry that I, too, was ruining her big moment. I grabbed her hand. "Your ring is beautiful — and so big, too! Everyone is going to be impressed."

At that, she started to brighten. "It is gorgeous, isn't it? It's the very kind I wanted. I had dropped some hints." She gave me a small kiss on the cheek, and ran to catch Peggy, who had just walked past us. As captain of the waitresses, Peggy had the honor of announcing recent engagements at the end of dinner.

As I watched Ellen so happily share her news with Peggy, someone tapped me on the shoulder.

"What's wrong, Sookan? Why are you looking so lost?" It was Marci, all dressed up in a tan silk dress, matching pumps, and white gloves. She had on a touch of makeup and her hair was slightly curled under.

"Marci, you're here! And all dressed up, too. What a day for surprises! First Ellen and now you."

"What about Ellen?" Marci asked.

"Oh, nothing. This is the first time you've come here for dinner, isn't it? You look beautiful."

"I do not! I feel silly. What a lot of fuss just to come and eat! I'd just as soon sit and read, but I wanted to see your candles. They *are* pretty. Did you light them all yourself?" Marci looked around awkwardly. "Where should I sit?"

"I know. Sit over there with Ellen and her gang. It will be fun at that table. And dinner is really good tonight: roast beef, and chocolate cake and cling peaches for dessert." I escorted her to her table as I carried a pitcher of ice water there.

After dessert was served, Peggy tapped on her water glass with a spoon. This meant only one thing. Everyone grew quiet. "Which senior is it?" people whispered. "Oh, this is always so exciting!"

I watched Ellen smile and look up at Peggy with anticipation just as everyone else did. I knew Ellen had dreamed of this for a long time. This was her moment. I saw how she had folded her right hand over her left, and sat very still.

"I have a very special announcement this evening,"

Peggy said. "A member of the freshman class has just gotten engaged."

"A freshman? Who could it be?" I heard the crowd buzz.

Peggy shouted over the swell of voices, "Ellen Lloyd is engaged to Kyle Spencer, a junior at Princeton. Marriage plans will be announced at a later date. All the best to you, Ellen."

Many girls ran over to Ellen's table, wanting to see her ring and hear all about Kyle, and the proposal. Ellen looked like Miss Universe, with everyone hovering about her in admiration.

She is so happy, I thought as I watched Ellen. The happiness she couldn't share with her family, she could share with friends. I wondered why families couldn't be more like friends and be supportive without always judging. I supposed it was impossible. With family, there was too much love, too many worries, and too many expectations. I thought of my sister and of all the plans she had for my life. Would I someday hurt my sister as Ellen was hurting her parents? Then I thought of Bokhi and Hyunchun. If they lived here, it might be possible for them to be together. I was caught between two very different cultures. *Would I be able to balance the two and create my own special world?* I wondered.

When I went back to my room that night, Ellen was sitting on her bed with a box of tissues. Her eyes were red and puffy and her hair was falling in her face.

"Ellen, what's wrong?" I asked.

"Sister Reed called to congratulate my parents. They immediately called me and were furious that I had announced my engagement to the school. They told me that I was to call it off and come home right away. But I'll show them. They can't hang on to me like that. Kyle and I need each other, and we'll be together no matter what they say. We're going to elope." She blew her nose and hurled the box of tissues onto the floor.

I tried to reason with her. "Maybe your parents are just worried about you. I don't think they're really angry. What does Kyle think about all this?"

"He's insulted and upset," Ellen said.

"When your parents see how happy the two of you are, they'll come around. It must have been a big shock for them. Maybe they just need to get used to the idea. Why don't you and Kyle go home and talk to them?"

"I am not going to subject Kyle to them. They have been horribly mean," sobbed Ellen.

"They love you, Ellen. You can't just run away and get married all by yourselves. Your parents want to be there, and I want to be there. I thought you said I could be the maid of honor at your wedding!"

"You don't understand. I'm their baby, and they'll never get used to the idea. Besides, once they get my report card, they'll be even more furious with me. I spent so much time on extracurriculars and visiting Kyle at Princeton that I failed French last semester. I don't want to study anyway. All I can think about is Kyle, and the life ahead of us. I just want to elope and get our lives started now!"

"Maybe you should talk about it with Sister Reed. She's quite wise, you know."

Ellen glared at me and shouted, "Sookan, she's the one who made it even worse than it was to begin with! She and my parents are probably plotting against me as we speak. I know she's on their side."

"Ellen, you know how charming Kyle is. Have him talk to your parents and win them over," I pleaded. "When they see how much he loves you, I just know they'll change their minds."

"Oh, Sookan, you don't know anything. You think we always have to do what older people tell us to do. You don't understand. I have my life to live. You're on their side anyway. Just leave me alone and stay out of it!" Ellen's voice had risen to a scream.

No one had ever screamed at me like that before. I was shocked and hurt. But, I suddenly heard myself screaming back at Ellen. "Why don't you grow up? A big engagement ring and a boyfriend don't make you an adult. Maybe you should try to understand your parents, and understand why they might be worried. Kyle isn't the only one who loves you; they love you, too. Did it ever occur to you that other people might have things to say that make sense? You're acting like a spoiled and ungrateful idiot!" I threw my books on the floor and ran out of the room.

117

Up in my private study, the bathtub, I sat down and drew the white plastic curtain closed. I was upset and ashamed. I had lost my temper and I had hurt Ellen. I didn't go back downstairs until I was sure Ellen would be asleep, and the next morning I tiptoed out of the room before she woke up.

Chapter Fifteen

Winter was slipping away, and brave yellow forsythia buds were heralding the arrival of spring, my favorite season. It always thrilled me to see tiny buds emerge from the brown weathered branches. Ellen, as head of the dance committee, was frantically planning the Spring Fling, just two weeks away. Boys from Princeton, West Point, and Georgetown were chartering buses to come up for the evening, and it was Ellen's job to make sure that everything went right. Kyle was planning to bring his roommate, Tom Winston, and Ellen kept begging me to come to the dance so that we could double-date.

I was relieved to see Ellen so happy again. She had taken my advice, and she and Kyle had gone to talk to her parents together. After a long conversation, they agreed to have an extended engagement so that Ellen could finish school. Ellen promised to spend more time studying. She no longer spoke of eloping, and in fact, she and her mother were already beginning to make plans for the huge wedding they would throw in three years. Ellen and I were both ashamed of how we had screamed at each other, but I knew Ellen was grateful to me, and I was happy that I had helped her.

Each time Ellen mentioned the Spring Fling, I just smiled and said nothing. I had already decided that I would go, but I wanted to surprise her. I would wear my cream silk dress and the pearl jewelry that Sister Reed had given me. On my way to the dance, I would stop by Sister Reed's office and surprise her, too. I had it all planned. I just needed to buy a pair of beige high heels to wear with the dress.

Ever since January, I had been working every Saturday at the administration building. To save money, I had purchased second-hand textbooks from upperclassmen at a fraction of the original price, and I was careful not to use too many notebooks. The books I could not buy from upperclassmen I read at the library. And not having time to write home saved on postage money.

I finally thought I had saved up enough money to go downtown and buy not only my shoes, but the leather purse for Mother, some books for my brothers, and a few things my sister had asked for. I would make up for what I had not been able to send at Christmastime.

As I headed toward the store to buy Mother's purse, I passed a little boutique with a most exquisite, black short-sleeved dress in the window. Made of velvet, it was fitted, with a square neckline, black satin trim on the hem and sleeves, and a braided satin belt with a tiny bow in the front. A small, black velvet purse hung on the shoulder of the mannequin. The dress was small, and looked as if it might fit me. Before I had even thought about it, I found myself inside the store.

A tall, silver-haired woman approached me and said, "Would you like to try that on, dearie?"

"Oh, no, but it *is* beautiful! I just want to look at it for a while. That's the kind of dress my mother would make for me," I rattled on. "It's so simple and elegant."

The woman looked me over, then said, "You're so tiny. What size are you — two or four? This is a four, but cut very small. It would probably fit you well."

I had no idea what size I wore; I had never bought a dress in America. I just smiled, not knowing what to say.

"Here, try it on. Let's just see if it's your size. Most of my customers are too big for this little dress." She took it off the mannequin and gently pushed me toward the dressing room.

It fit perfectly and felt so soft against my skin. The pearl necklace and wishbone pin would really stand out against the black velvet. Now the cream dress that I had been planning to wear seemed drab.

"Heavens," the saleswoman exclaimed as I exited the dressing room to model for her. "It looks as if it were made for you!" Her gray eyes twinkled as she examined the fit. I wished I could buy it, but there was no way I could afford it.

I was about to take it off when the woman brought me

the little purse and a pair of black patent leather high heels. "Here, just see how the whole outfit looks."

She led me to a three-way mirror, and I saw how stunning the ensemble was. The shoes made me look tall, and the purse added a touch of elegance. *Wouldn't Ellen be amazed to see me like this?* I kept thinking.

"I can give you forty percent off if you buy all three. This dress has been here for a while, and I don't think it will fit anyone else as well as it fits you."

I don't know what got into me, but I bought the whole ensemble, and was left with only two dollars to spare. I wasn't able to buy a single gift. I went back to my room with an empty wallet — and two large shopping bags. I immediately hid everything behind my old dresses. Ellen and I shared a closet, and I didn't want her to notice the outfit before the dance. She had seen every dress I already owned, so I had to be careful to hide this one way in the back.

On the night of the dance, I told Ellen that I was planning to stop by at some point. She wanted to do my hair and show me how to put on makeup, but I just laughed and told her that I didn't want to go to all that fuss. I would get dressed after I finished my reading, and would join her later.

As soon as she left, I began to prepare. I curled my hair, polished my nails, and put on some makeup. I slipped into my black dress and high heels, then adorned myself with my pearl jewelry. Pleased with this new look,

I walked over to Marci's room to show her. She was not in, so I left her a quick note saying that I was going to the dance. Then I headed to Sister Reed's office.

When Sister Reed saw me standing before her, she gasped. "Sookan, you are exquisite! What a stunning outfit. Is it new?"

I nodded. She gazed at the pin and pearls she had given me. "Dear, you look stunning! Now, go have a wonderful time. I am so delighted to see you finally attending a dance. It's about time!" Like a proud, loving mother, she watched me walk away.

I became apprehensive as I approached the dance hall and heard the laughter and music. I didn't know how to dance, and I wondered if I would even know how to mingle with college boys.

The hall was jammed, and everyone looked wonderful. The West Pointers were spiffy in their starched uniforms and spit-shined shoes, and all the girls looked so graceful in their flowing skirts as they twirled about the dance floor. Overwhelmed, I stood at the entrance for a minute. Ellen was at the punch bowl, and I watched the wave of surprise that washed over her features when she noticed me. "Sookan? Is it you?! Where did that dress come from? Who got you ready?"

"I know how to get myself dressed, Ellen," I said.

"You are wicked to shock me like this; I'm going to have a heart attack right here. You're so stylish! Kyle, where is Tom Winston? Oh, there you are, Tom. Come here. I want you to meet my roommate, Sookan." Ellen grabbed my hand and dragged me through the crowds, introducing me to all the men. I was amazed at how easy it was to talk to everyone. It was exciting to be surrounded by handsome strangers, and to talk and drink punch and listen to music. Now, I could see why Ellen liked these gatherings so much.

Ellen suggested that I dance with Tom, even though I had told her many times that I didn't know how. But, Tom stepped toward me and assured me it was easy. He gently led me to the crowded dance floor and, deftly putting his arm around my waist, he started to lead.

"See, you already know how to dance," he said. "It's as natural as walking or talking. Later, I'll show you some fancy steps if you'd like."

I didn't answer. I was getting a bit nervous dancing so closely. Suddenly, I felt hungry and weak. I realized I hadn't eaten lunch. "Do you think we could go taste some more of that punch Ellen made?" I said.

Ellen winked at me. I knew I had made her happy; it was important to her that everyone enjoyed her parties.

Later, Ellen suggested to Kyle, Tom, and me that we all go to the Hilltop for drinks. I had often heard of it; it was a favorite hangout on the hill behind campus. We agreed and all hopped into Kyle's car for the short ride there.

I'm not sure exactly what I had expected, but I was surprised by the dingy, dimly lit restaurant, with its old wooden floors covered with sawdust. The music was blaring, but everyone was talking and laughing, and the hamburgers and onion rings smelled terrific.

"Hi, Ellen, I've reserved a table for you," said a man in his thirties, whom I later learned was the owner.

Many of our classmates were there, with drinks in hand, talking animatedly. Some waved to me, obviously surprised to see me there.

"What can I get you?" the waiter asked me.

"A glass of orange juice, please."

"Sookan, they make a terrific screwdriver here," Ellen said. "You've got to try it."

"One screwdriver coming up," the waiter quickly noted. I had no idea what a screwdriver was, but I didn't object. I knew Ellen was determined to expose me to "the college experience." Besides, I knew it was important to her that I seem with-it in front of Kyle and Tom. But when the drink came, it tasted to me like orange juice that had gone bad and I sipped it slowly.

I talked mostly to Tom, who sat next to me and wanted to know all about my classes and my jobs. He had a friendly, boyish smile, and I enjoyed comparing my experiences to his at Princeton.

Ellen said I needed to refresh my drink, but since I didn't like the one I had, I asked to switch to ginger ale.

"Oh, no, how about a Tom Collins — in Tom's honor," Ellen suggested. This one was cool and sweet, and I drank it down as I talked.

When we left the Hilltop, Ellen tried to convince me to spend the weekend with her at her home. We would visit the boys at Princeton, she said. But my head was starting to pound, so I asked her to drop me off at the dorm.

Ellen gave me a hug, and whispered, "I'm so glad you came tonight. Promise me we'll do this again."

"Bye, Sookan. It was great to see you again," said Kyle.

Then Tom offered me his arm and walked me to the front door of the dorm.

"I really enjoyed this evening." He hesitated, then added, "I would like to see you again. May I call you?" He gently held my hand in both of his, and waited for my response.

Flustered, I faltered, then hurriedly responded, "Yes, well, I had a good time, too. Good night." I pulled my hand from his, and ran inside.

As I walked down the corridor, I saw that Marci's door was open. "Did you have a good time?" she called out. "You didn't see me, but I walked by and peeked from the doorway. I saw you chatting with a tall, very cute guy. Who was he?"

"Oh, Kyle's roommate," I said.

"He was your *date?*" Marci squealed.

"No, he wasn't my date. We all just went to the Hilltop together."

"He *thought* he was your date. I could tell," she said. "He liked you. Was he nice? Did you have a good time?"

"He was very nice. He even offered his coat when he thought mine wasn't warm enough."

"I bet he's going to call you soon."

"No, he won't. Well, actually, he might. But I don't have the time to spend another evening like tonight. I have such a headache," I said, rubbing my temples.

"What did you drink?" Marci asked.

"Orange juice and some punch. But they had funny names — I forget. One of them was called Tom something."

"A screwdriver and a Tom Collins! No wonder you have a headache. Ellen should have warned you that those have vodka and whiskey in them. You'll be okay in the morning."

"Vodka and whiskey? What are those?" I asked.

"Alcohol. Booze," Marci said.

"You mean I went out on a date *and* drank alcohol? That sounds so wild!" I said. "Actually, though, there was nothing wild about it. But if my sister ever found out, she would really think I was losing my values."

"Don't worry. You need to get away from your books, the library, and the nuns once in a while. You know, you surprised everyone. I heard the girls talking about how smashing you looked."

"They all think of me as a mousy bookworm. Lately, I have been, I guess. But it's because I still don't feel completely comfortable with English, and I have to study so hard to keep up with everyone else. Sometimes I fantasize about being a famous diplomat. I imagine that I am tall and glamorous, and that I can charm people into signing all sorts of peace treaties. Well, anyway, that's enough of that. Maybe I'm drunk!"

Marci followed me to my room and watched as I took off my shoes and removed my makeup.

"So, you did have a good time, didn't you?" she asked again.

"I had a wonderful time. In fact, I enjoyed myself so much that it scared me. If I keep doing this, my studies will suffer. But I just wanted to go once to make Ellen happy, and to prove to her that I'm capable of looking elegant and of having fun. It was extravagant of me. I spent all of my money on this outfit, and I didn't even get any gifts to send home to my family." I thought of the soft leather purse I still hadn't bought for my mother. "And I didn't purchase any of those things my sister asked for! If she ever found out that I spent all of my money on a velvet outfit and went out on a date and drank alcohol —"

"Sookan, you have to remember that you didn't do anything wrong. It's okay. You can't let your sister make you feel guilty about taking one little, harmless break. You deserved it!"

"It's funny," I said. "I know my mother would tell me it was all right. She would acknowledge that I had done something impulsive, but would say that it was okay. My sister, though, would criticize and lecture me. It's amazing how differently she and my mother respond to the exact same situations. Even to the same letter."

"What do you mean?" Marci asked.

"Well, I wrote my family a quick letter about how you and I made Korean food and had a little party here. My mother wrote back and said she thought it was wonderful that we had done such a thing. But my sister said that I shouldn't have dared to cook for foreigners. She said that it was arrogant of me to try, that I don't know how to cook, and that I probably did a great injustice to Korean cuisine. She said I should have done something more worthwhile with my time."

"That's ridiculous. Everyone loved it."

"When I was in Korea, I thought everything my sister said was right. But now I find that I don't always agree with her, and I resent the way she tries to control every aspect of my life. Then, as soon as I think those things, I feel guilty about being so disrespectful. Maybe it's just that I'm so far away, and I'm in a culture that she can't understand. Or maybe it's the difference in our ages. I don't know. I wish I could make some sense of it."

"I don't think it's any of those things," Marci said. "It's not distance or the culture that makes it hard to understand each other. Look at me: I live fifteen minutes away from home and see my parents once a month, and I still sometimes feel they are from another planet! I guess the age difference can sometimes make things harder; my parents and your sister are older and think they know everything. Maybe that's it. But you don't have those problems with your mother, do you?"

"Oh, no. My mother doesn't push me at all. She trusts

me. She always says she knows I'll do just fine. It makes me feel good to know she believes in me."

"Yeah, that's all I want. I just wish my father would try to understand me and would trust that I know what I want out of life."

"Yes, that's all I want from my sister, too," I agreed. "I wonder if she has any idea how important her approval is to me? Her letters haunt me. Every time I enjoy myself, I think of her, and wonder what she would be saying. Just like tonight."

"Sookan, she is not a good sister to you. She's making you miserable. You've got to tell her to stop trying to run your life!"

Marci had said this to me before. It had been shocking to me then, when all I could think about was how disgraceful it would be not to obey my sister. I would bring shame on her, myself, and my family. *How my brothers would chastise me,* I had thought. But now, I was slowly beginning to feel that I didn't always have to obey my sister. Just because she was older didn't guarantee that she had the right answer for me.

In Korea, I wouldn't have even dreamed of thinking this way. But maybe that was why I had wanted to leave home for a while; I had always felt constrained there. My brothers and my sister used to remind me constantly that I was too expressive, too sensitive, too direct, and too ambitious for a girl. Here, everyone encouraged and complimented me. *Am I becoming vain?* I wondered. *Is the problem with me, and not with my sister?* I was tired of waffling between anger and guilt.

"Marci," I said, "perhaps we should be more thankful that we have people who care about us. After all, strangers don't drive us crazy like this. Only people who love us can cause us this much pain."

"I suppose. All I know is that I can't wait to go to Greece this summer. My family suffocates me; I just need to get away for a while. Did I tell you I found a classics group that travels through Greece performing plays in ancient amphitheaters?"

She suddenly looked so excited. I was going to miss her during those three months. "I wish you could come with me," she said, seeming to read my thoughts.

"Me, too."

"Are you all set with your summer job?" Marci asked me.

"It's all been arranged. I'll be working on campus. A Gregorian chant program is scheduled for June, and students will be coming from around the world. I volunteered to help at registration, and to give tours of the campus during the first week. After that, I'll be working for Miss Mullen in the placement office. I'm going to try to apply some of the work hours to my scholarship hours for next year, and to save as much money as possible. My dream is to be able to send my mother and maybe even my little brother, Inchun, plane tickets so that they can come to my graduation and then fly back home with me."

"Well, set some time aside in August," Marci said, smiling. "When I get back, we can go visit my aunt in Philadelphia together."

We hadn't solved our problems, but talking had been a much-needed release. After Marci went back to her room, I took off my dress and hung it carefully next to my cream silk dress in the closet. It didn't look as elegant as it had when I first saw it in the store. I felt frivolous for having bought it. I should have done my duty first. The cream dress would have been fine.

While I was reprimanding myself, I heard Mother's voice. *Sookan, stop that. You are a bit impulsive and head-strong at times, but you did well.* I smiled, remembering how gentle yet firm Mother was. *Well,* I thought to myself, *I will work steadily at my job, and maybe by Easter time, I will have saved up enough to buy all the things I had planned to send home.*

I reached to unclasp the pearl necklace, when suddenly, the strand broke, and all the pearls scattered across the floor. On my knees, I scrambled to pick them up. I collected them from under the two beds, and all across the floor. After staring awhile at the handful of dust and pearls before me, I got out a handkerchief, and wiped off each pearl one by one. I remembered something my mother used to tell me. She used to say that women are like oysters. Just as an oyster takes an irritating grain of sand and creates a pearl around it, a woman can take a painful experience and enrich herself by creating something precious from that pain. We take in the misery and the bitterness, but instead of letting it poison us, we turn it into a precious pearl. Difficult times can make us rich within, as long as we remember the story of the oyster.

I cleaned each pearl and thought of my mother. She had suffered so much, and she had made herself richer for it. She was rich in understanding and love. Even now, when she was so far away, I could hear her stories, and they comforted me. I put all my pearls into a little box. The next day, I would find some thread, and restring the precious beads.

Chapter Sixteen

Freshman year was drawing to a close. I had taken my last exam, handed in my last paper, and felt confident that I would get passing grades. I looked up at the clear blue sky as I walked over to the art studio, my new favorite spot. Painting was the one course of the semester that demanded no work outside of class. Sitting in the sunny, spacious studio was relaxing for me. There, my mind wasn't racing to try to think in English. I could just concentrate on my painting and escape.

Everyone else had already cleaned out her drawer, and the cleaning crew had begun its work on the studio. I opened my large, flat drawer that held all the work I had done over the course of the semester. There were several charcoal still lifes of various collections of fruits, nuts, and flowers. They looked amateurish to me now. There was no sense of space and balance. The meticulous detail made each nut and piece of fruit look almost too perfect. Then I found some later sketches. One of them particularly pleased me. Three walnuts were scattered on a table, and one was cracked open, with the meat of the nut detailed. The strokes were graceful, not tight and cautious as in the other sketches. I had only meant to keep a couple, but I couldn't part with any of these sketches that had taken me so long to do. I took them all out of the drawer and put them into my bag.

I walked over to my easel, which held the painting I had just finished. It depicted a large, pink crystal vase holding a bouquet of white chrysanthemums. The sun shone through the window behind it, creating a brilliant rainbow reflection on the crystal. It would make a perfect gift for Ellen, as pink was her favorite color. The other painting I had done was quieter and more intense. It was of an apple, a pear, strawberries, and red grapes, all clustered together on a rustic wooden table. *Marci would like this one,* I thought.

I arrived back at the dorm. The last group of students was getting ready to leave, and their parents were busily trying to get things loaded into their cars. The doors to all the dorm rooms were left open, revealing spaces that were completely empty except for the beds and dressers, and the papers and hangers that littered the floor.

I went back to my room, expecting to see Ellen packing. But the room was half bare. There was a note on my bed.

Sookan,
    My parents and Kyle came early. I looked for you at the library, but I couldn't find you. Where

135

are you? Well, I have to be off. I'll call you tomorrow. Come spend the weekend with me — or the whole week if you can. My summer counseling job at Camp Piquanock doesn't begin for a while, so I'll be home and would love to have you visit.

Love, Ellen

P.S. Kyle told me that Tom Winston wants to see you. Why didn't you tell me that you two spoke on the phone a few times? He's going to be staying around Princeton for the summer, and maybe you won't be so busy.

I sighed. I liked Tom. I had had a wonderful time with him the evening we all went out, and I did want to see him again. But when he first called, I had grown flustered and heard myself explaining that I just didn't have the time to see him. He had said that he understood, but that he'd keep in touch. He called a few more times, but I never wrote or called him back, and I felt sorry that I might have hurt his feelings. It was true that I didn't have time to date, but I was also afraid. I felt that I didn't really know *how* to date, so I had decided to avoid dating altogether. I didn't want to say anything to Ellen, because I knew she would make me double-date with her again, and I didn't think I could handle that. Maybe my sister was right. Maybe I had left home too early.

I wished that I, too, could pack up my things and head back home for summer vacation. But Korea was too far away and the journey too expensive, so the college would be my home for the summer.

I had planned to give the painting to Ellen before she left, but now I was glad to have the chance to surprise her. I got out some paper and started to wrap it. I could almost picture Ellen's delighted reaction upon receiving this big package in the mail. I missed her already.

"What are you wrapping?" Marci said, poking her head into the room.

"Hi, Marci. Come in. I'm getting a painting ready to mail to Ellen."

"Oh, these are great. I love this one: the fruit looks so real," Marci said. "I wish I could draw and paint like you do."

"I was going to wrap that painting and sketch for you. Do you really like them?"

"I love them, but are you sure you want to part with them?" she asked.

"Oh, yes! They are for you," I replied, relieved that Marci liked my work.

"I already know where to take them to be framed, and I have the perfect spots for them in my room." Marci gave me a quick kiss on the cheek. Unlike Ellen, who left us all branded with her pink lipstick, Marci never hugged or kissed anyone. I was glad to see her being so expressive and spontaneous.

"Why didn't you give Ellen's gift to her before she left?" Marci asked. "There was lots of room in their big station wagon."

"I didn't get back in time to see her off. Her parents and Kyle came earlier than we thought they would."

"Oh, I see," Marci said. Then she added, "I can take you downtown to mail it. The college post office is already closed."

"Thanks, Marci. You're always there for me," I said, as I placed her thumb on the string I was trying to tie. "Oh, and can we stop by a couple of stores? I want to finally pick up some things for my family."

"Sure, I've got time," Marci said. "Listen, Sookan, after you do all that, do you want to come to Philadelphia with me to visit my aunt? We can spend two days there, and then drive back Sunday. I leave for Greece on Monday."

"Thanks, Marci, but I think I'll just stay here. I'm so tired, and I still need to pack up. I have to clear out of the dorm for a few weeks so the cleaning crew can do their job. Sister Reed has arranged for me to spend that time at the infirmary."

"You aren't sick, are you?" Marci asked, looking worried.

"Oh, no. I just need somewhere to stay, and Sister Reed thought it would be a good place to get some rest since it's so quiet there."

"Come on, let's take care of everything. Then we can go for a drive to Greenwich, and take a walk by the water," Marci said, lifting the package I had just finished addressing.

"In that case, let me take my camera. I must begin to take some pictures for my family," I said, digging the camera out of a drawer.

The sky was so clear, with only a few large, bright white clouds, just like a child's drawing. Sailboats basked lazily under the hot sun. Leaning back on a big dogwood tree, Marci and I stared out at the water. It was a sleepy afternoon, with the sun seeming to slow the whole world down.

"Marci, thanks for helping me with everything today," I said. "I feel so relieved after mailing that package home. I'd been wanting to do that all year. I do hope my mother likes the purse. I know that she places very little value on material things, but I wanted her to know that I was thinking of her. Maybe the gift was more for me than for her."

Marci pulled a small box from her purse and said, "Speaking of gifts, this is for you."

I carefully opened it. It was a beautiful gold bracelet. I just stared at it, so Marci took it out of the case and unclasped it.

"Look, I had an inscription put inside. 'To my dear friend, Sookan. With love, Marci. 1955.' "

I was speechless. Instead of thanking Marci, I gave her a big hug, and then sat admiring the bracelet through my tears.

"You have such small wrists," Marci said, putting the

bracelet on me. "I had to get the smallest one they had, but it fits you perfectly."

"Thank you, Marci, I love it," I mumbled.

"No, Sookan, I wanted to thank *you* — for being such a special friend. It was a hard year for me; I just didn't feel like I fit in and I didn't have any friends. But you changed that. And talking to you about my family has been such a help to me, too."

"I didn't do anything."

"Yes, you did. You understand people much better than I do. Much better than most people do, I think. Ellen said you helped *her* a lot this year, too. I helped her pack this morning and we talked for a long time. If it hadn't been for you, she said she might have eloped with Kyle. She said you really made her stop and think, and because of you, everything is turning out better than she had ever hoped. I like Ellen, now. I'm so happy the three of us are going to be roommates next year. Ellen's excited, too. And *you* brought us all together."

Embarrassed by her compliments, I fussed with my camera and said, "Marci, would you sit over there? Let me finally take some pictures of you."

We posed for each other until I had finished my roll.

"Next year, I'm going to take a photography class and learn how to develop my own pictures," I said. "My brother Hanchun was never willing to show me; he said it wasn't for girls." I imagined how magical it would be to watch a picture emerge from a sheet of blank paper.

Then my brother's image rose before me. Visions of home always appeared to me at the oddest times.

"You know," I said, "I might see if I can still sign up for a summer photography class. I think they have one in the evenings."

"I wonder if my father would show us how to process the film," Marci said. "We have a darkroom in the basement, and he still keeps asking me to use my camera. Maybe I'll try to take some good pictures when I'm in Greece. Actually, Sookan, don't sign up for the summer course. When I get back from Greece, we can learn together, okay?"

It was a wonderful idea. I smiled as I thought of how happy Marci's father would be. The sun shone warmly on my face and I closed my eyes. I realized I had dozed off when Marci shook me and pointed to her car. We drove back to campus, thinking our own thoughts. It had finally sunk in that I had made it through my first year, the year that Mother had been so worried about. It had been frustrating at times, overwhelming, and a lot of hard work. But it had been challenging and exciting, with so many new things to learn. It was a grand accomplishment.

This summer I would write long letters to everyone. I would write to each of my taciturn brothers, even though they had never written to me. I knew they were thinking of me and were just not very expressive. They had always been that way, yet I still wished they would write and tell me that they missed me and that the house felt empty without me. I smiled, realizing how silly I was being. They could never write that kind of letter. I leaned back and played with my bracelet. Marci glanced over at me and turned the radio on. We left a trail of soft music as we sped down the highway.

Chapter Seventeen

I went with Mr. and Mrs. Gannon to see Marci off to Greece.

"Thanks for coming to the airport with us," Marci said, full of excitement. "I still wish you were joining me. Now, don't go overboard with your volunteer work. Take a couple of days off before you begin your summer job, promise?" I assured her I would, and wished her a good trip. She had been dreaming of visiting Greece for so long, and I could see how exhilarated she was. Her parents looked nervous, but relieved to see Marci so happy and full of life.

When the Gannons dropped me off at school, I went over to Sister Casey's office to see what I could do to help. She asked me to write nametags in calligraphy, and to help register the students and give tours of the campus the next day. Despite my promise to Marci, I worked all week long. I told Ellen that I had no time to visit her before she left for camp, but that I would see her when she got back. I missed her already.

My job at the administration office turned out to be a

busy one. My days were filled with typing and filing. I worked until six, and often took envelopes back to my room to stuff. The more hours I fit in during the summer, the more time I would have to study during the next semester.

On my way back to my room one night, I stopped by the post office and found a letter waiting for me. I could tell it was from Inchun by the handwriting on the envelope. But when I opened it, I found that Inchun had only written a few words. He had enclosed a letter from Mother. It seemed strange, as I had prepared so many self-addressed envelopes for her.

Dear Nuna,

Mother and I thought we would write to you together for a change. It's hard to believe this is my first letter to you, when you're almost at the end of your first year at college. By the way, Father Lee may be going to America in the near future. He plans to visit you. I hope everything is going well at school.

Your little brother, Inchun

I grimaced in frustration after reading his short note. He had always been taciturn, but at least when I was near him, I could glean so much from his expression. I longed to hear what he was doing. I wished he would tell me that he missed me.

Mother's letter would be more heartening, I knew.

My dearest Sookan,

May must be a very busy time for you with all your papers and tests. I am praying that you do well. I know this first year has been very difficult for you so far away from home. I worry that you are trying to do too much, that you are trying to be perfect in everyone's eyes. Please give yourself the time to grow and to know yourself. Trust your heart. You are a young woman now.

If you ever feel hurt or tired or empty, I hope that you will remember what I have always told you about taking that suffering, and creating a pearl around the pain. Don't let the hurt poison you. Difficult times can make you rich and strong if you remember this lesson. It has always helped me. I think it has already helped you, as well. Your life has been hard, and you have come through all those difficult times enriched with enormous wisdom for someone so young.

By the time you receive this letter, I hope that you will be getting some much-deserved rest, and will get to have some fun with your friends over summer vacation. Father Lee is going to visit America, and if he is in New York, I know he will try to see you.

I am always with you.

Your loving mother

Her letter was dated May 1, and Inchun had not sent it until the 30th. Confused, I stared at the sheet of paper. They had never written together like this before. Of course, there was no reason they shouldn't — or wouldn't. Still, I wondered if something was wrong at home. Was Inchun trying to hide something from me? Mother usually mailed her letters right away. Besides, the tone of her letter was somehow different.

Maybe she was simply worried because she hadn't heard from me in a long time. I felt guilty for not having written during the entire month of May. I had been swamped with papers and exams. And I had wanted to send a letter full of good news after I had gotten through everything successfully. I guess Mother knew I was struggling to finish the year.

I began to write Mother a long letter, telling her that I had completed all my exams and papers, and had officially gotten through my first year of college in America. I told her all about Ellen's intense romance, Marci's departure to Greece, our plans to all room together next year, and my full-time job at the administration office. As soon as I finished, I walked across the empty, moonlit campus, and dropped the letter in the mailbox.

The next day, I filed and typed all morning. I was on my way downstairs for lunch, when I saw Sister Casey.

"Sookan," she said, "I was just coming to look for you. You have a visitor here all the way from Korea."

"Father Lee? Already?"

"He had some church business in Philadephia, and he stopped in to see you before heading to Rome."

Sister Casey looked strangely solemn, and I started to worry. "Has he been here long, Sister?"

"About an hour. He spoke with me, and with Sister Reed. We both wanted to tell him how proud we are of you. He was so happy to hear that you are doing well here." She smiled and placed her hand on my shoulder, and we began walking down the marble stairs to the sitting room on the first floor.

When I had received Inchun's letter, I thought I would be excited to see Father Lee. But suddenly, I felt frightened. I wondered if Mother was all right. I looked at Sister Casey, but she seemed to be avoiding eye contact with me.

Father Lee was sitting with Sister Reed, and as I entered the sitting room, Sister Reed stood and opened her arms to greet me.

"Here she is, Father Lee. Our pride and joy. Sookan, we will let you visit with Father Lee. Sister Casey and I will be in the next room. We'll see you later, all right?" She smiled, but I saw the concern in her deep green eyes.

I bowed deeply. "It's wonderful to see you here, Father Lee," I said. Then, abruptly and ungraciously, I asked, "Is there something wrong at home?" I hadn't even thanked him for taking the time out of his busy schedule to come see me. I was too nervous. I needed to hear him tell me that everything was okay.

"Sookan, why don't we take a walk?"

I shook my head. Something was wrong.

"Father Lee, if you don't mind, I would rather talk here. Is my family all right? Has something happened?"

He motioned to the seat across from his and I sat down, waiting for his answer. His black suit was crumpled, and he looked tired and drawn. Watching his every movement, I waited impatiently for him to speak. He wrung his hands, and cleared his throat.

"Sookan, I am sorry that my first visit with you has to be such a sad one. I came here because I wanted to tell you in person. Your mother . . . your mother has joined God in Heaven," he said almost inaudibly.

I wasn't sure that I had heard him correctly. Had he really said that Mother had gone to Heaven?

"But I just got her letter. She only mailed it two weeks ago."

"Sookan, I know it's hard to believe," he said, "but your mother is now with God."

"You mean Mother is dead!" I shouted, jumping to my feet. "She is dead, and no one told me until now!"

He stared down at his hands, then looked up at me helplessly. "I am sorry, Sookan."

My head started to pound. I sat, buried my face in my hands, and sobbed.

Father Lee poured me a glass of water and handed me his handkerchief.

I wiped my eyes. "When did she die, Father?"

"On the first of May," he answered.

"But she wrote to me on the first of May."

"Sookan," he said, sighing, "your mother was hospitalized in mid-April. She had fainted, and they found out it was a cerebral hemorrhage. After about twelve days, she seemed to be improving. She was doing nicely for a few days, and we were all hopeful that she would fully recover. It was during that short period that she spoke to your sister and brothers. She asked that they not tell you anything until your summer vacation began. She said they must let you finish your first year without worrying about everyone at home. She wrote you a letter during that miraculous time. We were all there. She asked In-chun to hold on to the letter and to send it later with a note, so that you wouldn't worry. Then, she asked me to bring you these things in person. She seemed so lucid and strong, but she knew she was dying. She finished what she wanted to say, and then slipped into a coma. She died very peacefully. She seemed to be smiling when she died, as if someone had come to welcome her."

I held the small package that Father Lee had brought me. It was wrapped in a blue silk scarf that Mother had made. She always made scarves out of remnants of silk, saying that scarves always came in handy. She would stay up hemming the edges late into the night. She didn't need any light to do this type of sewing, and she liked staying up and looking at the moon. There had been so many nights when she had stayed up sewing to keep me company as I studied.

As I numbly played with the knots in the scarf, Father Lee talked about Mother. "She was the most amazing woman I've ever known. I have always loved her as if she were my own mother, and she always treated me just like a son. She was so gentle and yet so strong. So wise, and yet humble. She had a hard life, but she was always there to help and comfort others." He paused. "There wasn't room in the church for all the people that came to the funeral. The whole town was there, weeping. In all my years as a priest, I have never seen anything like it. So many people loved and depended on your mother. In-chun mentioned that she liked the mountains, so we buried her high above the city."

I didn't speak, and suddenly, I didn't even have the energy to cry. I just sat, thankful he was there and wishing he would never stop talking. I think he knew, for he continued.

"You know, Sookan, what made your mother so special was her ability to accept people. She firmly believed that one was born with one's nature. One could try to change but would ultimately remain the same. Because she believed this so firmly, she appreciated people for their strengths. She managed to overlook their weaknesses and never criticized them. She also believed that each person was born with a destiny. She never tried to impose her will on any of her children. She wanted each of you to pursue your own path. Until the very end, she wanted to make sure that you had your chance. She didn't want anyone or anything to stop you. She wanted you to live your own life and, most of all, to be happy. I think you know that."

Sister Reed came in and invited Father Lee to have some lunch and to stay at the college for a night. He thanked her, but said he must leave soon to catch his plane to Rome. He bade her goodbye.

"Sookan, your mother wouldn't want you to be sad, you know that. You have to make yourself happy and successful for her. That's what she wanted."

I nodded and wiped my tears in silence.

"I will come see you again," he said, and quietly left.

Clutching the small package, I stared at the spot where Father Lee had last stood. I couldn't believe that Mother was dead and buried. It was too much for me to bear. I ran to my room.

There, I opened the little package. In a silk pouch that Mother had made was her thin, white gold wedding band. I put it on and pictured the ring on Mother's hand. How busy her hands had always been, cooking, gardening, and sewing for all of us.

Despite what Father Lee had said, I stayed in my room and cried for the rest of the day. Why had I left? Mother hadn't wanted me to leave. No one had. Why had I been in such a hurry to come to America, just when Mother needed me most? I hadn't been a good daughter. I had been selfish. My sister had been right in all of her letters. I remembered how sad Mother had looked when I boarded the plane. That was only ten months ago. Why hadn't I waited just a little longer? I should have been there to talk to her that last time. Why, I hadn't even sent her that little present in time! I kept reproaching myself over and over again, and cried myself to sleep.

Several hours later, I awoke. The crescent moon was high in the sky. It was fuller and brighter than the night before, and yet the world had turned black for me. I sat on my bed for a long time, feeling helpless, then walked toward my desk and took out Mother's letters, all nine of them. I hugged them and cried. As I began to read them one by one, her words brought her voice to me. I could almost see her tired but peaceful face, wanting to pass on all the support and wisdom that I needed from her. In each letter, she told me she was proud of me. She told me not to worry about things at home. She wanted me to be happy.

Even in her final letter, it was clear that she wanted me to have the confidence to focus on my work and on my new life here. She didn't want anything to defeat me, not even her death. That's why she told me about the pearls, again. She didn't want me to lose hope. I had worked hard to settle in here, and Mother had worked hard to make sure that I had that chance. I couldn't let it all go to waste. I would pull myself together. I would struggle to form another pearl within me. Clutching her letters, I fell back to sleep.

Chapter Eighteen

The following morning, I rose with the sun and attended six-thirty Mass. Then I went to work, and finished the filing that was left. Sister Reed stopped by to see me. She told me that she would like to hold a Mass in memory of my mother that afternoon in the main chapel. After the Mass, if I wanted to get away for a while, she would arrange everything for me, she said. I thanked her for the kind offer but told her I wanted to stick to my summer plans.

At the Mass for my mother, Sister Reed sat next to me in the front pew. Sarah and Jimmy, all dressed up, sat to my right. Professor and Mrs. Bennett were close by, as were Sister Casey and Miss Mullen. Ellen and her parents were there, as well. Ellen peered at me through tear-filled eyes, and I quickly turned away for fear that I would start to cry uncontrollably. I bit down hard on my lower lip. Looking behind me, I saw Marci's parents, Peggy Stone, all of the nuns, and the rest of the administration office staff.

I was touched and grateful to everyone who had come,

but I was too numb even to acknowledge them. Everything seemed so unreal to me. I felt as if I were floating in midair watching someone else attend the Mass. I just sat there as Father Fleming spoke. I couldn't even recite the prayers.

As I stared forward listlessly, little Sarah snuggled up against me, and whispered into my ear, "I love you, Sookan." She squeezed my hand.

Suddenly, tears filled my eyes and I couldn't swallow. I tried to clear my throat, and said, "I love you, too, Sarah." I held her hand tightly.

How precious children are, I thought. *What power their innocence has.* Sarah had brought me back.

When the Mass was over, I was able to muster a smile and thank everyone for coming. Mrs. Bennett asked me to spend a few days with them, and the Gannons and the Lloyds also asked me to come and visit. Mr. Gannon told me he had phoned Marci and that she would be calling me soon.

Ellen pulled me aside and hugged me tightly for a long time. "I am so sorry, Sookan. Please tell me what I can do to ease your pain. Please tell me. You look so pale! Come home with me for a few days."

I pulled away from her tight embrace. I was afraid that if I began to cry again, I might not be able to stop. My family would not like me to make a scene. I stood tall and said, "Thanks, Ellen, maybe later on. I can't right now; I have to work. But how is everything? How is Kyle?"

"He is fine, and everything is fine. You are the one I'm worried about. Kyle sends you his prayers, as does Tom. The two of them wanted to come with us, but I told them not to. I wasn't sure if you would want to see them now. Oh, Sookan, please come home with me. I miss you."

"Thanks, Ellen, but I really can't," I replied.

"You are so stubborn, Sookan. Why won't you let me help you for a change? You've always helped me. You're the one who made me work things out with my parents. You're the one who made everything turn out all right for me. Let me help *you* now!" she implored.

Then Peggy Stone stepped up and embraced me. "I'm working in the city, now," she said. "Here is my address. When you feel up to it, come visit and we will go up to the top of the Empire State Building. You should see all the lights from there! I know how you always loved seeing all the candles glow in the dining room." I listened and nodded at her gentle attempt to cheer me up.

I thanked everyone again, but said that I just wanted to be by myself for a while. Perhaps I would visit everyone later in the summer.

For the next few weeks, I got up at dawn every morning and joined the nuns in their morning prayers before Mass. I was comforted by their high-pitched hymns reverberating in the domed chapel.

After Mass, I worked at the office without a break until five o'clock. I needed to have something to keep my hours and days filled. I felt detached from reality. It was as though I had been separated from my body. I felt as if my body were going about my daily tasks all on its own, tending to all my work, and smiling and chatting and getting through the day. But at night, I was alone in the quiet of my room. I was alone with my grief. Huddled in a corner, I cried and cried. *I'm an orphan now*, I kept thinking. I was all alone in this big world.

After a few weeks, I finally remembered to check my mail, and found a small package from Inchun. I slowly read his letter.

Dear Nuna,

I thought you might want to have Mother's reading glasses, so I am sending them to you. Father Lee told us about his visit with you and the nuns. He said Mother and all of us would have been so proud to hear what the nuns had said about you. I'm not surprised. Mother knew, too. She was always very proud of you.

It is still so unreal to me. Life seems so meaningless. But I know Mother would want us to pick ourselves up, and carry on. I can still hear her voice in my head telling me what to do. In that sense, she is still with me, and I am grateful for that. I'm going to study hard, and keep my promise to her to become a good doctor. I only wish I were a doctor already so that I might have helped Mother when she was sick.

She told no one about her illness, and then she suddenly fainted one evening. Who knows how long she suffered alone? When Mother came to, she emphatically told all of us that she did not wish you to hear any bad news from home until you had finished your freshman year. She wrote her last letter to you in the hospital and told me when to mail it. I think she knew then that it would be the last letter she would ever write to you.

You know that she wants you to continue your studies in America and fulfill your dream. That would please her. Do it for me, too. Please do not come home until you finish your studies. We are all doing okay here. There is nothing you can do for us. So don't worry, and take care of yourself.

Your little brother, Inchun

I stared at Mother's glasses for a long time. Sending them was Inchun's way of telling me he knew my sorrows and was thinking of me. Tears streamed down my cheeks. He needed me, and I was not able to comfort him. Now, it was my little brother who was comforting *me*. He should have kept Mother's glasses. He was the one who had stayed with her. I wished I could be with him. We had come through so much together, and I felt terribly alone without him during this difficult time. I pushed his letter deep into my pocket.

As the weeks wore on, I received postcards and letters

from Marci, phone messages from Ellen, flowers and cards from Kyle and Tom, a box of cookies from Marci's mother, drawings from Sarah, and a sympathy card from Jimmy, which his mother must have bought for him. Ellen's mother sent me pink pajamas with a note that said, "I am always here if you ever want to talk or visit. Hope it won't be too long until we see you." I was grateful to all of them for caring so much about me. I would write them sometime, but not now.

No letters came from any of my older brothers. I wished they would write. I wouldn't have cared what they said. I just needed to know that they were thinking of me, and that we were all going through this together. I wanted to scream and shake them. I needed them to say something — anything — to me now.

But I was being silly, I realized. They couldn't share their pain with me. They had to appear strong and dignified. They couldn't let their little sister know how sad and helpless they felt. I knew that each of them probably cried at night when no one else could see. I knew how they must hurt. But they would not write or call until they felt they were strong enough to be of help to me. I understood, but it hurt me all the same.

One day I found a small envelope in my box. The handwriting was Bokhi's.

Dearest Sookan,

Forgive me for not writing to you all this time. The first few months after you left, I was

over at your house often, and your mother filled
me in on your life in America. But then, life
changed for me. Perhaps your mother told
you. I am now engaged to a man who my family
believes is a perfect match for me. I am sure
I will learn to love him. I have met him, and he
seems to be a good man. I trust my aunt's
judgment.

How can I express my feelings at this
tremendous loss. I loved your mother as if she
were my own. After you left, I felt she had sort of
adopted me as her new daughter, and I was so
happy being with her.

My aunt and I attended the funeral. The whole
neighborhood was there. The church was packed,
and people were standing in the doorways. People
were wailing and beating their chests shamelessly.
I was too sad and numb to even cry. Why must
such a lovely person die so early? How could her
kind God do this? Now, I am full of bitterness. I
know your mother would scold me, but I can't
help it. Everyone I love has been taken away from
me, time and time again. Sookan, how I miss you
and wish you were here!

I will write again. Our paths are now different,
but I know you love me and I will always love
you. I cherish our friendship. Be well and be
strong.

                                    Your best friend, Bokhi

Hidden behind Bokhi's letter had been one from my sister. I decided to wait, and put the letters in my bag. When I got back to my dorm room, I reluctantly took out my sister's note.

Dear Sookan,

I grieve for Mother and I pray for her night and day. Although you have not taken the time to write to me personally, I have been following your life as best I can from reading your letters to Mother.

As soon as Mother fell ill, I wanted to write you. How worried our brothers and I were about Mother, and how we wished you had been here. But during that short period of time when Mother was able to talk to us clearly, the most important thing she wanted to tell us was that we should not disturb you until you had finished your first year of school. I hope you realize how deep her love for you was.

Mother's death was very peaceful. She was smiling as she slipped away. But how we all wept as she left us. Our brothers cried for days. I am still crying. I cannot believe Mother is gone. I remind myself that she is in Heaven with God.

Now that Mother is gone, it is you and I who must look after our brothers. Our responsibilities are greater than ever before. We must make sure that they are taken care of, and have all that they need.

When the coffin was being lowered, many of our relatives and neighbors took off their lace veils and placed them on the coffin. It was a lovely gesture. Lace is very expensive here, and it was dear of them to part with such prized possessions. I would like you to replace their veils for them. I will send you their names and addresses.

After the burial, we spent hours fixing mother's tomb. We even went back the following day to do more work. Her tomb is on the top of a hill overlooking the Han River. It took us so long to climb up and down that my legs are still sore. It was a sad two days of planting flowers.

I pray that you are well and that God will bless you with peace.

Your loving sister

I regretted that I had not been at Mother's side for the past ten months. I wished I had been there to talk to her at the hospital. If only I could have attended her funeral and helped to decorate her tomb. I still could not comprehend it all. As I read my sister's letter, it still sounded so unreal to me.

I took a deep breath and thought of my mother, who was always so gentle and calm. *I must get hold of myself,*

I kept thinking. But I couldn't. I missed her, and I couldn't stop thinking about her.

I felt at once guilty and sorry for myself for not being with the rest of my family to share the sorrow with them. I could tell that my sister resented my absence. I was hurt that she did not understand how painful it was to be away from my family during such a difficult time.

But I remembered what Mother had always said about not being able to change someone's nature. Father Lee was right; that was one of Mother's fundamental beliefs, and because of it, she accepted all of us for what we were. Mother understood my sister, and accepted her. But it was clear now that Mother also knew how my sister demanded things of me. That was why Mother had asked everyone not to disturb me until the end of the school year. It was uncharacteristic of Mother, for she almost never interfered in our relationships with each other. She usually trusted each of us enough to let us handle our own affairs. But she knew that the news of her death would overwhelm me. She wanted to make sure she had taken care of everything for me before she died.

I realized I must accept my sister, as my mother had done. Nothing would change her, not even Mother's death. I saw now that she had her own shortcomings, insecurities, and anxieties. It was my responsibility to try to understand her as a human being. I was older now. I had to realize that no one was infallible. I could respect Theresa without obeying her blindly. And beneath it all, I knew she cared for me in her own way and was doing the best she could. No matter how hard I tried, I could not sever our familial ties. She was my sister, and we were bound by my mother's love for us.

As I had done so many times before, I took out Mother's last letter to me. I reread her words of encouragement and trust. She knew how I would feel, and did not want me to be consumed with sorrow and bitterness. She wanted me to turn my pain into pearls of wisdom and understanding. "Tough times are the times when one gathers one's pearls," I remembered hearing Mother say to me long ago, as we worked together in the kitchen. I would make myself stronger within, I resolved, and then, perhaps, I could be more forgiving and accepting of my sister. That would make Mother proud, I thought. I would do as she wished for me. I would gather my pearls and forge ahead. I would finish college and figure things out from there. I didn't know what my future would bring, but I would do as Mother had always told me. I would follow my heart.

With new determination, I piled up all the letters I had received from home and wrapped them tightly with the blue silk scarf Mother had made. I put them deep into my desk drawer. There, I saw the little box of loose pearls, still waiting to be fixed. Feeling resolute and newly calm, I sat at my desk and began to restring my pearls.